*The
Kidnapping
of
Aunt
Elizabeth*

Barbara Ann Porte

The Kidnapping of Aunt Elizabeth

Greenwillow Books, New York

The excerpt from "Gimpel the Fool" from
Gimpel the Fool by Isaac Bashevis Singer,
Copyright © 1953, 1957 by Isaac Bashevis Singer,
is reprinted by permission of Farrar, Straus
and Giroux, Inc., and Jonathan Cape, Ltd.

Library of Congress Cataloging in Publication Data
Porte, Barbara Ann.
The kidnapping of Aunt Elizabeth.
Summary: Ashley finds a unique family portrait
evolving as she talks to family members and
collects their stories for a class assignment.
1. Children's stories, American.
[1. Family life—Fiction] I. Title.
PZ7.P7995Ki 1985 [Fic] 84-18757
ISBN 0-688-04302-X

This book is for my sisters,
Carolyn and Eloise

. . . the longer I lived the more I understood that there were really no lies. Whatever doesn't really happen is dreamed at night. It happens to one if it doesn't happen to another, tomorrow if not today, or a century hence if not next year. What difference can it make? Often I heard tales of which I said, "Now this is a thing that cannot happen." But before a year had elapsed I heard that it actually had come to pass somewhere . . .

Isaac Bashevis Singer
—*"GIMPEL THE FOOL"*

CONTENTS

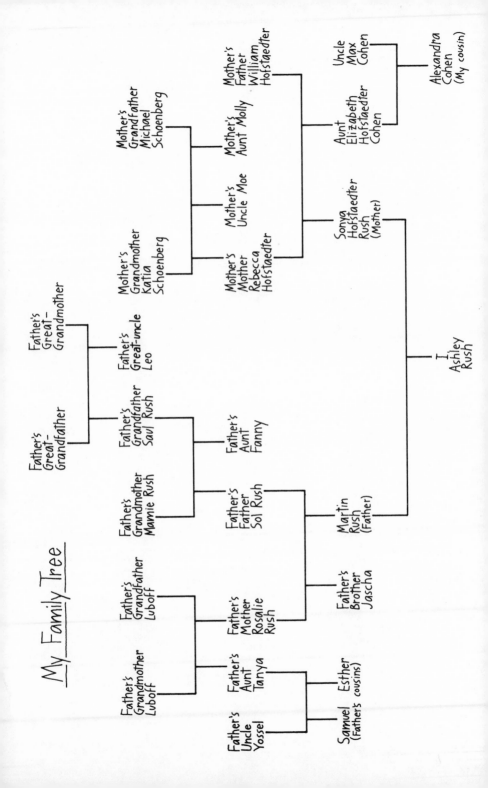

*The
Kidnapping
of
Aunt
Elizabeth*

Social Studies, I

"Family history project?" I sit up straight and pay attention. Can it be she's joking? Of course she isn't joking. If you knew Ms. Baxter, then you'd know she doesn't ever joke.

I go to the front of the room after class and stand at her desk. "Can I do something else?" I ask when she looks up. "I mean, instead of family history. Anything else."

"Don't be silly, Ashley," says Ms. Baxter. "You will do the family history project, the same as everybody."

"Please," I say. "I can't. I'll do two reports instead, if you'll just let me."

"Ashley." Ms. Baxter stares at me with more than her usual interest. "Have you some special problem with this particular assignment?" As though I'd tell her if I did.

Still, I have not attended school ten years for nothing. It dawns on me what she is thinking. I could tell her anything. My mother ran away from home when I was four. When I was five, my father joined the circus, an aerial act. I was brought up by my grandparents on my father's side until they took up the trapeze.

"No," I say. "No special problem."

"I'm glad to hear that, Ashley."

I continue standing there.

Ms. Baxter sighs. "Is there something else?"

"Is family history like a family tree?" I ask, knowing full well that it must be. "Because if it is, my parents won't approve." That much at least is true.

When I was in fourth grade, we had to do a family tree. I was the only one in my entire class to have to make mine up, from scratch, entirely. It was the most humiliating experience of my life, up to that point. I was sent to the principal's office because my family tree was so interesting.

⊂ 2 ⊃

"Is this really your family tree?" the principal asked, impressed.

"No," I had to say. "I made it up. My father helped me."

In fourth grade I still believed telling the truth was essential. My mother had to send a note. Goodness knows what she wrote. It was in script; only now we call it cursive. I can still hardly read my mother's cursive. For a fourth grader it would not even have been a remote possibility. But I could imagine.

"We," she very likely would have written, meaning to include all relatives on both sides of the family as far back as Adam and Eve, "do not believe in making public that which is personal and private. We especially do not believe in it for a school assignment."

What she said at home out loud was: "Where do they come off asking children to spy on their parents?"

"It isn't spying," I tried explaining at the time. In fourth grade I sided with any teacher, against all odds. Nowadays I am reluctant to believe anything I hear in school. "Columbus discovered America," I have heard from more than one source. It is a mistake to trust what comes only from a textbook.

"Suppose," my mother said, unwilling even then to let any subject drop unfinished, "families have secrets they do not care to share with the rest of the world?"

"Have we any secrets?" I asked, interested.

"Don't be silly," she replied. "Besides, that isn't the point. *Some* families might."

"Not my family," Father had said. "My family doesn't have secrets. Tell about them. You can say that we're descended from King Solomon." My father's name is Sol.

"Are we really?" I asked.

"Please," Mother said.

"She's just jealous," Father explained, "because her family isn't as interesting as mine."

"King Solomon," I printed carefully at the top of my page.

"And Queen Sheba," said my father. "Don't forget Queen Sheba."

"Queen Sheba," I penciled in as neatly as I could.

"You don't understand," I tell Ms. Baxter now, hoping to enlighten her. "It isn't possible to tell one's family history when one's family history is a secret."

"You'll just have to do your best," Ms. Baxter tells me. "I'm sure you'll think of something."

I can see there is no point in trying to discuss it further.

CHAPTER 2

The Kidnapping of Aunt Elizabeth

"Tell me about the time Aunt Elizabeth was kidnapped," I ask my mother after dinner. She is sitting, feet tucked under her, on the kitchen chair, with Luther, the cat, in her lap. She has on a long blue robe, held together with a sash. It's what she wears when she's at home, or another one just like it. When Mother is not at home, she usually is dressed for work. Mother is a biochemist. She works in a laboratory. It is the same laboratory where Father works, although they work in different parts of it.

Both of them leave the house every day dressed alike, in crisp white lab smocks and trousers. Mother wears oxfords, shoes that can be walked in, as she puts it. At lunchtime she does not eat lunch. She takes walks instead. That explains her extreme thinness, which I try unsuccessfully to duplicate. Father usually works through lunch.

"Why not?" he says. "I like what I do."

Mother looks at me. "Don't you have any homework, Ash?"

"It is homework. It's for social studies class." I explain to her about my family history project.

Mother sighs, probably remembering fourth grade and the family tree. "I guess," she says doubtfully, "it wouldn't hurt to put it in a project. It is a sort of family story. Although," she adds, "I would think there'd be more important things to learn in school."

Father lifts his eyes from his newspaper. "I didn't know Elizabeth was ever kidnapped."

"Not really kidnapped," Mother replies. "You know how Ash likes to exaggerate."

I can hardly believe she said that. It happens in my family I am the only one who understands there are important differences between real and make-believe. "I think," Grandma Hofstaedter told me once, "it comes from working in a laboratory."

Grandma Hofstaedter is a lawyer, though retired, and entirely practical. "Scientists deal every day in miracles. It can't help affect their judgment. They come to think that everything is possible. We," she said, including me, "know better."

"Face it, Ash," my cousin Alexandra used to say, "the family is peculiar." She meant it democratically, including relatives on every side. "Haven't you ever noticed," she still asks from time to time, "that only you and I are normal?" It sometimes seems to me, especially of late, that Alexandra is right.

Alexandra's mother and mine are sisters, identical twins. It is to that circumstance I've always attributed their oddities. Father's peculiarities, on the other hand, I blame on the fact that he is an only child. "So are you, Ash," he reminds me. "So are you." Don't think it doesn't worry me.

Mother pours herself a cup of coffee, then waits for Luther to settle down again. "She wasn't really kidnapped, Ash," she tells me, meaning Aunt Elizabeth wasn't. "We only thought so at the time."

"You thought so?" I ask in amazement. "How could *you* have thought it? It was you who arranged it." I have heard this story before, though never the same way twice. If Mother tells it enough, I think one day I'll hear it right.

"Your mother said what?" Alexandra has asked

whenever I've tried to get the details straight. "What did she say?"

"Nothing," I say, "never mind."

My way is never the same way she has heard it.

"We were only five," Mother is quick to remind me, as if it were an explanation. "By the time the police arrived and our description was being broadcast on the radio, I had begun to think that what everyone was saying was true."

"They put your description on the radio?" I ask.

"Her description, my description, it was the same description. We only meant it for an April Fools' Day joke."

"Some joke," says Father.

"It was all Lucy Locket's idea anyway," Mother continues, "even though Elizabeth and I were the ones to get punished. We wouldn't even have known about April Fools' Day if she hadn't told us."

"Lucy Locket?"

"Well," Mother says, "we always called her Lucy Locket lost her pocket. Her real name was Luckett. She lived across the hall. On the day of the kidnapping we had played all afternoon in her apartment. It was exactly like our own. Had Lucy's mother been at home that day, the apartment would have been too hot to play in."

When Father looks up, Mother explains what I

already know. "The apartments all had fireplaces, but hardly anybody used them. The rooms were too small to accommodate the heat. In our own fireplace we had electric logs. Lucy's mother, though, had real logs in hers, and any time that she was at home, she lit them. When the apartment was hot enough to suit her, it was too hot for anybody else, including Lucy. Grandma always thought she did it on purpose. 'She'll put up with anything except for children,' she would complain to Grandpa. Still," says Mother, "she was nice enough to us when she was there.

"When she wasn't there, Hildegarde was. Hildegarde was hired to watch Lucy. Hildegarde also kept pigeons, though not in Lucy's apartment. She had her own apartment by the East River, and sometimes she would let us all visit her there."

One of Mother's worst memories, she once told me, was the time when she, Aunt Elizabeth, and Lucy killed Hildegarde's favorite pigeon by spraying insecticide all over the kitchen. Even years later, telling me, she sounded remorseful. "We weren't even punished. Everyone said it wasn't our fault, that we were only children and didn't know any better. Of course, we knew better. They said it was careless of Hildegarde to leave the spray bottle where we could reach it, that if there was any fault at all, it was hers.

Oh, how we longed," Mother said, real longing in her voice, "to be punished."

"I never longed," Aunt Elizabeth tells me later when I ask her, "to be punished. It was punishment enough to be known throughout the neighborhood as a pigeon killer, even though your grandmother always did add when repeating the story, 'Of course, they didn't know what they were doing.'"

The important thing about Hildegarde, however, that Mother likes to recall was that she slept in a nightgown with nothing on underneath. By morning the nightgown would have crept up around her shoulders, and she, Hildegarde, would be lying in bed totally naked. "Your grandmother," Mother would say, "always slept in pajamas and made Aunt Elizabeth and me do the same. 'If it doesn't keep you warm,' she would ask, 'then what is the point?'

"Other children that we knew," Mother informed me once, "were not allowed to play with Lucy on account of her mother's being an actress."

"Just because of that?" I asked.

"Well," Mother said, looking uncertainly at Father, "there are actresses and actresses."

"Exactly what kind of actress was she?" Father asked. But Mother changed the subject. Despite what Father sometimes thinks, she isn't really one to tell a child everything she knows.

Lucy, it seems, had learned about April Fools' Day in school that year for the first time. "It was news to us, to Aunt Elizabeth and me," says Mother, "but Lucy was a year ahead, already in first grade, and she explained it." Apparently, during the explanation, Hildegarde was in the kitchen, doing something about dinner. "She didn't actually make meals," Mother says. "She sort of assembled them." It was Hildegarde who taught Mother how good baby custard from a jar can be for supper. Mother still eats it that way, from the jar, especially when she feels tired or unwell. I used to be embarrassed finding it on the grocery list, having to pay for it at the supermarket, knowing that we had no baby.

Mother starts now to enumerate the events of that day, more or less in order as they happened.

"Lucy said good-bye to us, very loudly. Good-bye," Mother says, raising her voice to show how, causing Luther momentarily to raise his head and briefly to interrupt his purring.

"'Good-bye, good-bye,' Aunt Elizabeth and I called back nearly as loudly. We wanted to be certain, you see, that Hildegarde would hear. Then," says Mother, "I went home.

"Aunt Elizabeth, on the other hand, did not. She walked instead into Lucy's mother's walk-in closet, slipped behind a red silk robe, and stayed there. She stayed there for a long time. 'It seemed that days must have passed,' she told me afterward.

"After dinner, after Lucy's and Hildegarde's dinner, that is," Mother continues, "Lucy took your Aunt Elizabeth a piece of buttered bread and some cake and fed it to her in the closet. Some of the butter," Mother recalls, "came off on the red silk robe and left a stain that unfortunately never did come out, not even after it had been dry-cleaned twice.

"When it was dinnertime at our house," Mother says, "your grandmother said to me, 'Where's Elizabeth? Tell her to come to the table.'

" 'She's still at Lucy's,' I said. It was the truth.

" 'Probably,' Grandma answered, 'she is having dinner there.'

" 'Probably,' I said. We often did eat dinner at each other's houses, though, as I've said, dinner at Lucy's was nothing at all like dinner at ours.

"When bedtime came, Grandma said, 'I can't imagine that even *they* would let her stay so late.' 'They,'" explains Mother, "was the collective term Grandma used to indicate anyone resident in that apartment, permanent or otherwise. Letting us play with Lucy by no means signified her approval of the household.

" 'Sonya,' your grandmother told me at last

[Sonya being my mother's name], 'go and fetch Elizabeth home, please.'

"I went across the hall and rang the doorbell. Lucy opened the door. Hildegarde, who was just leaving, and Lucy's mother stood behind her. 'Is Elizabeth here?' I asked.

" 'Elizabeth,' said Hildegarde, 'went home hours ago. Hours and hours ago. I thought you both went home together.'

" 'Oh, no,' I said truthfully. 'I went home alone. We thought Elizabeth was still here.'

"By now your grandmother had joined me in the hallway. 'Isn't Elizabeth there?' she asked, worried. 'Well, then, where can she be?' Lucy and I shrugged. The grownups exchanged anxious looks. Grandma went back into our apartment to telephone Grandpa at his drugstore. It was just around the corner. He closed it up and came home in a hurry. It's the only time I can recall he closed the store when it wasn't closing time.

" 'The important thing is not to worry,' he said, sounding worried. Even then," says Mother, "I really couldn't understand why, with Elizabeth gone, he would think *that* was the important thing.

" 'I am sure,' Grandpa said, 'there is some logical explanation. A child doesn't just disappear walking from one apartment to another on the same floor of the same building.'

" 'You wouldn't think so,' said Grandma.

"Of course," says my mother, "Elizabeth was prone to accidents. We did all know that." Even I knew that. It was Aunt Elizabeth who was forever falling off monkey bars and swings, scraping her knees on the pavement. Otherwise stationary objects seemed to fall on her with regularity. Her legs bore scars even then from run-ins with escalators, car doors, one time a moving train. It was Aunt Elizabeth who once had ridden Lucy's brand-new birthday bicycle into the lake in Central Park, having just learned to ride, but not yet learned to stop.

"In any event," Mother says now, "this time was no accident. Grandma called the police. She didn't really have much choice. New York," she says, "is a very big city. Anything can happen.

" 'Don't worry,' the police said when they came, sounding unworried. 'She probably just decided to take a little walk. You wouldn't believe how many times a day this happens.'

" 'Ummm,' said Grandma, not believing.

" 'What does she look like?' they asked.

"Grandma pushed me in front of them. 'Like that,' she said. 'She looks just like that.' The police looked at her, then at each other.

" 'Twins,' Grandpa explained. 'They're identical twins.'

" 'Oh,' said the police, looking relieved, though it seemed to me they had no reason. They hadn't found Elizabeth after all, just someone else who looked like her.

" 'We'll just take a little look around,' the police told Grandma.

" 'I will help you look,' she said, and did.

"Grandma organized the neighborhood. Everybody looked. Lucy's mother looked; all the neighbors looked; the man from the fish market on his way home stopped to look. The lookers walked for blocks and blocks," Mother says, "around the neighborhood just looking. 'Her name is Elizabeth,' they explained. 'She's only five.' No one remembered having seen her.

"Well, of course, how could they have seen her in Lucy Locket's mother's closet behind a red silk robe? I am only repeating what I heard," says Mother, "about that night. By then I was already tucked in bed and crying. 'One twin up and missing is enough,' Grandpa said, tucking me in."

"Crying, why were you crying?" I ask.

"To this day," Mother says, "I don't know if I cried because I knew by then how much trouble we were in for playing such a trick or if I cried because in all the noise and the commotion I'd actually come to believe Elizabeth might have been kidnapped.

"'By a crazy,' someone had whispered in the kitchen earlier that night. 'Who else would do a thing like that?'

"'You're making me crazy' was something Grandma was forever telling Elizabeth and me. Suddenly in bed that night it came to me that what she meant to say all along was 'You're crazy, do you know that? You're both just a couple of crazies.'

"Hours went by," says Mother. "It was after midnight. Grandma was in the kitchen making coffee. She made coffee in every emergency I can remember. Grandpa was pacing up and down in the living room. That was when the doorbell rang. It was Lucy's mother. I don't know," says Mother, "whether I was more afraid by then they'd find Elizabeth or that they wouldn't. Either way I knew it wouldn't be pleasant.

"Lucy's mother had Aunt Elizabeth by the hand. 'Hard by the hand,' as Aunt Elizabeth put it later.

"'Is she all right?' Grandma and Grandpa shouted, rushing to retrieve her, as though Lucy's mother had been the abductor all along.

"Lucy's mother's low, theatrical voice carried into my bedroom, where I stopped crying long enough to hear what she was saying.

" 'It seems,' she was saying, 'it was an April Fools' Day joke, cooked up by the girls. My Lucy hid your Elizabeth in my closet. They only pretended she was leaving. After dinner Lucy got Elizabeth from the closet and put her in her bed. When I went to check just now on Lucy, I found two girls instead of one underneath the covers.'

"Finding out that Lucy's mother checked on her at all surely came as a surprise to Grandma. Actually it came as much of a surprise to me. When Elizabeth and I were in our beds, our mother did not check on us. Except when we made noise. 'Stop making noise,' she'd say then, 'or you'll be sorry.' "

Mother sets Luther down on the floor and brushes off her hands. "That was that," she tells me.

"What do you mean, 'that was that'? Tell me what happened afterward to you and Aunt Elizabeth."

"Your grandmother came into the room later that night when we both were in our beds, both of us crying, and said in her soft voice, 'You girls haven't heard the end of this, believe me.' We believed her. 'We'll discuss it,' she told us, 'in the morning.'

"The police came in the morning. Grandma served them coffee and bakery danish and listened while we apologized for our behavior. They told us if not for our age, and Grandma's being a lawyer, they surely would have had 'to take us into custody.' As it was, they said, they'd let us stay at home on good behavior and in our mother's keeping. They would check on us, they said, from time to time. For an entire month, besides, we were not allowed to play with Lucy. Lucy got to play with anyone she liked. 'I hope you girls have learned your lesson,' Grandma kept on saying."

"Had you?" Father asks.

"I guess, so far as April Fools' Day went. I can't remember that we ever played another joke. Still, it left a lot of other days."

I start to leave the room.

"Ashley," Mother calls behind me, "if you use my story in your project, be sure you change the names."

"Change the names?" She must be joking. "It's supposed to be about my family," I remind her.

"Change them anyway," she tells me. "No one in your class will have to know." She turns on the water to wash the dishes. There is no point in arguing. She wouldn't hear me. She'd only say, "Sorry, Ash, the water's running. I can't hear you."

CHAPTER 3

Father's Russian Tale

I t seems as though social studies class has come to dominate my life. It is not so much that I am hard at work on my project as that worrying about it is taking up so much of my time. Nor is it as if I have no other classes to prepare for, but I am the sort of person who finds it hard to concentrate on more than one thing at a time. "You must get organized, Ash," Mother is forever telling me. "Put your life in order. For goodness' sake, at least clean your room."

By Sunday I am beginning to feel desperate. That

may explain my temporary lapse in judgment. I ask my father to tell me a story about someone in his family. You might think by now I would know better.

"You did what?" Sylvia says to me later when I tell her. "You asked your father to do what?" Sylvia Lee has been my best friend since kindergarten. She remembers my fourth-grade family tree. "Oh, well," she says, having thought it over, "if nothing else, it should be interesting."

"It needn't be *that* interesting," I remind Father when he starts his story, "just so long as it's the truth."

Father looks a tiny bit hurt. "I may not always get every detail right," he replies with a straight face, "but I do not lie." I don't bother to remind him of King Solomon. "For all we know, that is the truth," he'd say, and anyway, I want to hear his story.

"It is about my father's father," he begins. "His name was Saul." Without meaning to, I sigh.

"His name was Saul, and he lived in Russia. On a farm," he adds, watching me carefully.

I reach for a pad of paper and a pencil to take notes. "Don't forget to take notes," Ms. Baxter told us, "or use a tape recorder." Father continues.

"It wasn't a really big farm, but it wasn't such a little farm either. As farms go, it was somewhere in between. The summer Saul was eight, his father, your great-great-grandfather, gave Saul a newborn calf to be his own, to take care of and rear. Saul could not have been more pleased. He took very good care of that calf. He planned to show it at the village fair the following year. He hoped it would win a prize. Well, that was what he hoped and planned before his brother Leo, your great-great-uncle Leo, got hold of him and gave him a brand-new idea.

"Your great-great-uncle Leo," Father explains, "was quite a few years older than Saul. He would have been a teenager that summer. What he told Saul was that if Saul wanted, he could train himself to pick up a bull, just like that, to lift a full-grown bull, which that calf was going to be in just a few years, and carry it around in his arms. Wouldn't people in the village be surprised? Well, at first Saul did not believe him. He knew how much a full-grown bull weighs."

"How much?" I ask. "How much does it weigh?"

"A lot. It weighs a lot." Father sounds impatient. He does not like to have his stories interrupted.

"The thing Saul had to do, Leo told him, was to make sure that every single day of its life he lifted up that calf and held it. He wouldn't have to hold it for even a minute; half a minute would be enough, more than enough. The important thing, Leo warned his brother, was that if he missed even one day, the plan wouldn't work.

"The idea," Father explains to me on the chance I might not otherwise get it, "is that if you lift a growing animal each day, as it gets bigger you'll get stronger, a day at a time."

"And Saul believed that?" I ask.

"Why wouldn't he?" Father answers. "Leo was older. He knew much more than Saul did, and certainly more about bulls. You would have believed it, too, when you were Saul's age. I certainly believed it," he says.

"You believed it? You weren't even there."

"That's how much you know," says Father. "Why can't you ever wait until the end of a story before interrupting?"

Waiting until the end would not be interrupting, but I don't point this out.

"In any event, the important thing was that Saul believed it. He became very enthusiastic about the plan. After all, there had never been a person, much less a child, whom he had ever heard about, not only in his village but in all Russia, who could lift a full-grown bull and hold it. Why, he could charge people just to watch him do it. He'd get rich. He'd be famous. That's what he thought. And for a time at least," says Father, "the plan did seem to be working.

"Every day Saul would go to the barn and pet his calf. He'd speak to it."

"In Russian?" Mother asks, coming into the room and sitting down on the sofa.

"Of course in Russian. They were in Russia; what else would he speak? After that Saul would bend over and pick up the calf. Even at first it was hard. I mean," he explains, "a baby bull is still a bull. It isn't as small as you might suppose. Besides, it has four long and spindly legs that fly in every direction and a tail that does not stay still. Also," he adds, as though he had been there and seen it, "a calf does not care much for being lifted, not even by the one who feeds and waters it. Saul, however, was persistent.

"Every day for weeks that summer he would go to the barn and pick up his calf. Sometimes Leo would come by and watch. 'You're doing fine,' he would encourage his brother. 'Won't folks be surprised?' He meant, of course, surprised when the calf was full grown and Saul was walking around the farm with a bull in his arms."

Father pauses and smiles to himself.

"Well, what happened?"

"What happened was Saul came down with the

chicken pox. That's what happened."

"They have chicken pox in Russia?" Mother asks.

"Sure they have," Father says. "They just call it something else."

"What? What do they call it?"

"How should I know? I'm not Russian. Besides," he says, "that is not an important part of the story. The important part is that one morning in the middle of summer Saul woke up and didn't want any breakfast. His mother touched him on his forehead and said, 'You feel a bit warm, even for summer. I think you must be coming down with something. You had better stay indoors until we find out.'"

"Did she make him a guggle muggle?" Mother asks. I want to know that, too.

I used to think that guggle muggles were something Father had invented. But no. One day a few years back Mother had come across a woman at work, a chemist from Russia, who also knew about guggle muggles. Only she made hers differently.

Father's were made with warm milk, a little brandy, and some honey. He would float a pat of butter on top and give it to me to drink whenever I was sick. Sometimes just the thought of one would be enough to make me well.

"No wonder no one ever wants to drink yours,"

Mother told him, having discussed the subject with the Russian chemist. "You make yours wrong." Dr. Hauptman, it seems, made hers mostly with raw eggs. It did not seem to me to be a great improvement, but Dr. Hauptman said they were delicious. She remembered that in Russia her mother made them for her as a treat when she had been especially well behaved. The eggs would be stirred in a pot with lots of brown sugar to make a paste. A little whiskey would be added. It would be eaten with a spoon. At least, I thought, there was no mention of the awful pat of butter.

"Probably," says Father, "his mother made Saul a guggle muggle and tucked him in bed. By dinnertime, however, what he had was no secret. Saul was covered with spots. 'Chicken pox,' said his mother. Of course"—Father looks hard at Mother—"she said it in Russian. 'I guess,' she said, 'you won't be going anywhere for a while.'

"Saul fretted and fretted. But it wasn't any use and it didn't do him any good. His mother saw to it he stayed in bed. She brought him food and told him stories, but she absolutely, positively would not hear about his getting up and going out of doors and certainly not to take care of his calf. 'Your brother, Leo, will see to it fine,' she told him. Of course, she didn't exactly understand the situation. A week went by."

Father sighs, but behind his glasses his eyes are glinting as they do when he is pleased with himself. "By the end of the week," he says, "Saul was all better and his spots were nearly gone. Naturally the minute that his mother allowed him to go out of doors, the very first thing he did was run to the barn. He petted his calf and spoke to it. Then, very slowly and very carefully, he bent over and placed both his arms around its middle. He tried to stand up. He tried and tried. He pushed and pulled. He grunted and strained, but it was no use. Try hard as he might, he could not even begin to pick up that calf. A calf, you see," Father points out quite unnecessarily, "grows more in a week than a person who isn't a farmer might think."

"Exactly how much does it grow," I ask, "in a week?"

Father shrugs. "I'm not a farmer," he says. "In any event, your great-great-uncle Leo came by just at that point and said to my grandfather, 'What did I tell you? You can't say I didn't warn you. I told you every day, you have to pick up the calf every single day, or else the plan won't work. Missing even one day would have been too much. And you,' he pointed out, 'have missed an entire week. Maybe,' he said, walking away, 'you can try again next summer with another calf.'

"He hadn't counted, however, on Saul's persistence. *'Nyet,'* he called out after Leo. 'A week's not so much. It's just that I've been sick. I'm still a bit under the weather.'"

"Under the weather?" Mother raises an eyebrow.

"'You'll see,' Saul said. 'When I've got my strength back, then I'll do it.' He wouldn't let himself believe," says Father, "that he was not ever going to lift that calf again. It took an entire week more before he let that fact sink in. And when it did"—Father smiles—"was your great-grandfather ever angry! Until the day he died, he insisted that if he only hadn't contracted chicken pox that summer, he would have been world famous, or at least famous in Russia, as the only child ever to have lifted up a full-grown bull and held it in his arms."

"Is that a true story?" I ask.

"Of course it is."

Mother frowns. "I didn't know Saul lived in the country. Didn't you tell me once he lived in St. Petersburg?"

Father seems to be thinking. "I believe you're right," he says in a while. "It must have been Saul's father who lived on the farm."

"I thought Saul's father was the one who owned the jewelry store." Mother also can be persistent.

Father rubs his chin. His eyes get back their glint. "Now I've got it right," he says. "Saul lived in St. Petersburg with his father, who had the jewelry store. It was Saul's grandfather who had the farm. Saul sometimes visited him there." Father is watching me to see if I believe him. I gave up taking notes at chicken pox.

"Saul kept a bull in the city?" Mother asks.

"It wasn't actually a bull." Father lowers his gaze. "I just said that to make a better story, for Ashley's project. It was kopeks. Saul and his father saved kopeks in the back room of the jewelry store. Bags and bags of kopeks." Father spreads his arms expansively to show how many bags. "Bags of kopeks can be very heavy. As heavy as a full-grown bull," Father says slyly, "if you have enough of them. Saul and his father had enough.

"They started out with just one sack when Saul was little. It was a small sack. Every day Saul would pick it up. Then they'd add a few more kopeks. The next day Saul would pick it up again. Each day they'd add maybe a handful of kopeks. One kopek a day, it would have taken them years," Father says. "More time than they had."

"Time for what?" Mother asks.

"Time for Saul to get strong. Saul's father

wanted him strong for the trip."

"What trip?"

"The trip to America. Saul's father knew he'd need to be strong. It was a long way to come on a boat, carrying everything you owned, when you were only eight."

"Are you sure?" Mother asks. "Are you sure it happened that way? I thought Saul was grown up when he came."

Father thinks some more. "I think you may be right," he says. "It wasn't Saul. It was his son. It was my father, Sol, all along. He was the one who had to get strong."

"Grandpa," I remind him, "was already living in America when he was eight. [It will turn out I am wrong.] In America, there are no kopeks."

Father slaps the arm of the chair in which he is sitting. "Right again," he says. "What could I have been thinking of? They were pennies that they saved all along. Grandpa saved bags of pennies in the basement of the house where we were living in the Bronx."

There is a funny cracking sound. It is the sound my pencil makes as I break it in half. I thank my father for his story. Tomorrow, I think, I may go to the library, clean my room, jump off a bridge. I will not think about my father's Russian tale.

"Don't think about ghosts and you won't have bad dreams," Alexandra once told me Mother used to tell Aunt Elizabeth at night before they went to sleep. Aunt Elizabeth, to this day, suffers nightmares. "Ghosts walk in my sleep," I have heard her complain.

CHAPTER 4

Taking Notes

The Monday following the Sunday on which I heard Father's story of the bull, I do in fact go to the library. ("Bull story," "cock-and-bull story"— "bull," not a bad word. "Bull" in the dictionary originates not only from *bula*, "a steer" and *bhel-*, "to swell up," but also from *boule*, Old French, "a lie or bragging statement," leading me further to discover that "bully" was once used to mean "friend." Then, when friends hanging around street corners together in England began to beat up those passing by, "bully" came to mean what we called Cynthia in grade school, a petty tyrant whom we ran away from. "You have to stand up to people like that," our mothers kept telling us, without telling how.) The reason for my going to the library is that research, much to my surprise, is part of our assignment.

"Research is an important part of your assignment," said Ms. Baxter halfway through our class today. "When you hand in your project notes, in addition to the outlines of your stories, I expect to find solid evidence of careful research."

"Research?" I whispered to Sylvia. "What project notes?"

Sylvia shrugged. I could see it came as news to her as well as me.

"There are books in the public library on family history," Ms. Baxter went on to inform us, although it turns out she is wrong. "Preliminary outlines, including research and a bibliography, in proper form, are to be handed in two weeks from today. Is that clear?" In view of the ensuing silence, I suppose Ms. Baxter had every reason to assume it was.

At the library I look in the catalogue drawer. Four titles appear under the subject heading "FAMILY HISTORY." Not one is on the shelf.

"I can't understand it," says Ms. Randall, the librarian. "Books on family history hardly ever circulate."

"It's for a class assignment," I explain.

"Oh, for a class assignment," she repeats dully. "Well, what can one expect then? If only," she says, "someone would tell me beforehand. I would put books on reserve."

"Don't worry," I say in a tone meant to console her. "It isn't your fault." Ms. Randall has helped me with assignments since first grade. Also, I happen to know for a fact, there are at least four people in my class who do not consider it beneath them to telephone home before school ends on the day of an assignment so that their mothers can hurry to the library and take out everything there is on the subject. Well, you are allowed only four books on any one topic, only two should the librarian happen to know beforehand it is for a class project. Of course, like today, she does not usually know until it turns out all the books are gone from the shelf. "If only," she always says then, "someone had told me." There are, besides, some mothers who will take out-of-school siblings with them to the library; that way each mother and each sibling may borrow two, and sometimes four, titles on whichever subject. Doing so not only provides their own children with the information, but sees to it the rest of us won't have it.

"Just because there are such people," Mother says when I complain, "doesn't mean we have to be like them." What she means is, even if she did not work and had the time, she wouldn't borrow books for me for my assignment.

"If the library were computerized," I suggest to Ms. Randall, "perhaps that would help." The library is unmistakably old-fashioned. When I was eleven or twelve, not that long ago, books on sex education, even just on menstruation, could not be borrowed on a "juvenile card" without "parental permission." Since everybody's parents already knew this information, the books were always in, sitting unread on the parents' shelf. The rule has since been changed, though not in time for me. I'd had to write away for pamphlets from public-minded sanitary napkin companies. Naturally I shared the information thus obtained with Sylvia. Mother, of course, is a liberated person, not to mention a scientist. She would have been more than glad to tell me anything I cared to ask. But some things, I find, I would as soon discover for myself.

"Like sex," Sylvia said, closing her eyes and refusing to watch the family living film shown last month in health class. "There are things," she said, "I'd sooner be surprised by."

"Computers," Ms. Randall informs me, "are not what we need. Computers register only what's here. The more money spent on computers, the less money we'd have to buy books. We have little enough as it is. There'd be fewer family history titles, not more, on the shelf." She says it with authority. I don't point out fewer than none is not possible.

Ms. Randall, by the way, is beautiful, although naturally older now than when I met her for the first time years ago. She is medium tall and slender, with dark blue eyes and curly hair worn short now. When I was in kindergarten, her hair hung below her shoulders and was almost black. Now it is slightly streaked with gray. Also, in those days she sometimes brought her guitar to work and played it, singing folk songs with the children. In summer she wears sandals, but now she has on oxfords like my mother's. Perhaps she, too, takes long walks at lunchtime. I have heard, although I am not certain, that one year she ran in the city marathon and finished. She smiles a lot, except for times like now when she has trouble finding what is needed. What her private life is like, I cannot say, nor is it any of my business. It is, however, rumored that at one time, although not recently, she earned extra money belly dancing on the weekends. Watching her as she moves along the bookshelves, I find it is not hard to believe.

"Music librarian," Sylvia once told me. "She used to be a music librarian."

"You could look up family history in an encyclopedia," Ms. Randall suggests to me now.

"We're not allowed." No encyclopedias, Ms. Baxter warned us.

Ms. Randall sighs, the familiar sigh that she has sighed through all the years that I have told her this. "I do not understand," I have heard her say, though not to me, "what sort of reference work precludes the use of reference books. Never mind," she tells me. "It isn't your fault." She taps a pencil against her teeth, then says in a brighter voice, "Surely it need not *say* 'Family History' for you to use it." I follow as she walks briskly to the section labeled "Fairy Tales and Folklore." My father, I think, would be at home here. I am not convinced I will be helped.

"Folks who told these stories took them to be history. Try them," Ms. Randall says, handing me a stack of books. "They may surprise you."

I take them to an empty table and sit down. It is true I am surprised. I am surprised, for instance, to discover, in a book of creation myths, a story about first woman with teeth in her vagina. Teeth were how she controlled the world. It was man who one day tricked her and man who has been uncontrollably in charge ever since, according to the story. I do not write down this source.

"Always write down the source," Ms. Baxter tells us, "even when you think you may not use it. It is easier to write it down in the first place than to change your mind and have to look it up later." I am so certain, however, that I will not use this story that I do not even put it in my notes. Ms. Baxter, I think, would very likely not see its point. "But what is the point, Ashley?" I can just hear her ask me.

I examine the rest of the books in front of me, none of which seems exactly what I need. Still, a bibliography requires titles, relevant or not. Also, I do not care to hurt Ms. Randall's feelings. I select two, take them to the circulation desk, and check them out.

Later, at home, I sit in the middle of my bed and read them carefully. They turn out to be more interesting than I at first supposed. Whether or not they will qualify as family history is another matter altogether. I begin to take notes, hoping for the best.

Donald Ward, ed., *The German Legends of the Brothers Grimm*, Vol. I (Philadelphia: Institute for the Study of Human Issues, 1981).

I selected this book not only for its bright green

cover but also because glancing through its index, I saw, "Mandrake root, stories of."

It so happens there is a phrase which I have heard in my head, on and off, through the years, like a line from a song. "Get with child a mandrake root." I don't know what it means or why I hear it.

I copy the story for my notes, more or less the way I find it. "Taking notes is not copying verbatim from a book." I have been told since at least fourth grade that copying verbatim is plagiarism, which is as bad as stealing. Taking notes, the way I understand it, means to rearrange the order of the words before you write them down, substituting synonyms as much as possible. Of course, it doesn't make sense.

Notes from the "Mandrake Root," pages 93–94.

Legend has it when a thief was hanged but was innocent, only confessing under torture or, according to some, if his mother had stolen when pregnant, thus relieving him of the blame, if that so-called thief watered the ground where he was hanged before he died, then a mandrake plant, also known as a gallows manikin, will grow from the earth at that spot.

The mandrake plant, according to the legend, has broad leaves and yellow flowers on top. But one may not remove the plant from the earth without great danger, for if it is pulled up, it will groan and howl and scream so frightfully that the person removing it will soon thereafter most assuredly die or come to great grief.

To remove the plant safely, one must do the following: Before sunrise on a Friday, stop up one's ears with cotton, wax, or pitch; take an all-black dog with not even a single white hair on its body and go to the gallows site. Make three crosses over the mandrake plant. Then dig a ring all around it so that the roots are only barely attached to the earth. Next, take a long string and tie one end to the mandrake and the other end to the dog's tail. Show the dog a piece of bread and run off with it so that the hungry dog will follow, pulling the roots from the earth as it goes. The dog, which will not have stuffing in its ears, will then hear the groaning cries made by the mandrake, and therefore, it is the dog that will die. One must then wash the mandrake clean in red wine, wrap it in red and white silk, and place it in a small chest. But that is not all. For now the owner of the mandrake is obliged to bathe it every Friday and at each new moon provide it with a new white shirt.

The power of the mandrake is such that it will answer any question its owner asks of it. It will reveal the future and also tell how to attain prosperity and good fortune. Its owner will always be well off and never have enemies. If the owner has no children at the time ownership is assumed, a child will be born soon thereafter. If one leaves a bit of money with the mandrake at night, by morning the money will be doubled. However, one must not be greedy and overwork the plant or expect to double money every night or too much at any one time, nor should one expect a child each year or ask for twins. If one does, the plant will die.

When the mandrake's owner dies, then the youngest son will inherit it, but only if he remembers to place a piece of bread and some money in the casket with his father before burial. Should the youngest son die first, then the oldest son will inherit the plant, but only if the youngest also was buried with the bread and money.

I stare at the pages that contain the story. I like the story, but I don't know why. The ending disappoints me. Why should only sons inherit such a plant? I change the ending for my notes.

If the owner should die, I write, the youngest daughter will inherit the plant, and if she should die first, then the oldest daughter will inherit it. If there are no daughters, then the sons will get the plant. The problem of no heirs, of course, will not come up since whoever owns the plant is certain to have children. It's in the story. I wonder briefly about owners who are not married or who don't want children, but then I see it isn't likely they would go to so much trouble to obtain the root or put coins and bread in caskets to inherit it.

I open my second book.

Steven J. Zeitlin, Amy J. Kotkin, and Holly Cutting Baker, eds. *A Celebration of American Family Folklore: Tales and Traditions from the Smithsonian's Collection* (New York: Pantheon Books, 1982).

"Family tradition," it says, "is one of the great repositories of American culture [containing] clues to our national character and insight into our family structure." I write it down. It sounds impressive. I wonder, though, where it leaves Father's Russian story, if in fact it *is* a Russian story. "Family stories"—I continue reading—"are usually based on real incidents which become embellished over the years." Won't Father be glad to hear that? I think. "EMBELLISH," I write down in my notes, in capital letters, in the event Ms. Baxter doesn't know it. I pick out the story in the book I like the best, and I embellish it.

Notes from the "Sandbox," by Pam Matlock, pp. 134–135 (EMBELLISHED).

One time there was a little girl, maybe six. She lived with her mother and father not too far from the beach. This girl, as it happened, had a sandbox in her backyard, but it had no sand in it. The reason there was no sand was that the girl had a cat, and if there had been sand in the box, then the cat would have been sure to use it as a litter box.

Now, if there is anything more useless than a sandbox with no sand, I don't know it, and neither did that girl. So naturally every time she went to the beach—and that was every weekend in the summer, except when it rained—she would bring back a pailful of sand, hoping to fill her box. She was only six and did not understand at first how many summers it might take and that by the time she got the sandbox filled, she'd be too old to want to play in it. Still, she was smart enough for her age, and by the time several weeks had gone by it did cross her mind that it was taking a very long time to get enough sand in the box to make any difference.

Therefore, the next time the little girl went to the beach, and while her parents were sleeping with towels over their faces so as not to get sunburned (you'd think, going weekly as they did, they might by now have bought, or at least have rented, a beach umbrella, and don't you know that was the cause for many and many an argument, but that is not an important part of the story), the little girl took the key to the car trunk from out of her father's bag, which she was supposed to be watching for him. It also contained some money, not too much, but enough for hot dogs and gas to get home should more gas be needed. She unlocked the trunk and began to fill it with sand. You can imagine how long this would take, a bucket at a time. She worked all afternoon, meaning she left her parents alone for a change. They slept all day and woke up with terrible sunburns, which did not improve their dispositions any, you can believe me.

It was for that reason they left the beach a bit earlier than usual, and no one talked to anyone else all the way home. Well, almost all the way home, because part of the way the little girl's father noticed the car was wobbling and he said out loud, "As soon as we get someplace where we can pull over, I'll have to get out and have a look at the tires." But then after a while the car wasn't wobbling any more, so he never did stop and get out, and the reason, of course, was that the sand had started to dribble out of the trunk when they crossed over the bridge.

Of course, the first thing the little girl did when they got home was to get her father to open the trunk, and that was when she discovered her sand was all gone, except she could see a few places on the driveway where the sand had dribbled out even at the end. The little girl took her bucket and shovel and started to pick up the sand, as much as she could; as you can imagine, that could not have been easy.

The upshot of the story, according to the book, was that the little girl found herself all the way back at the beach trying to collect her sand, and of course, she hadn't the least idea how to get home. Her parents called the police to find her, and they did, and it got into the newspaper, and people read about it and felt sorry and sent the little girl sand. They sent so much sand that the sandbox was filled, and then some, and her parents had to pay to put an ad in the same newspaper telling the people not to send any more sand. And that was the end of the story.

I put the book aside and think about it, trying to decide what made me like the story in the first place. "Analyze your stories, class," Ms. Baxter told us. "Try to figure out what made them good enough to last." Analyzing almost ruins it for me.

It is, in the first place, a pretty dopey story. It is unlikely, to begin with, that a six-year-old, even working all afternoon, could fill a car trunk with sand. It is even more unlikely that her father wouldn't have had to open up the trunk before they left the beach to put away the towels and the suntan oil. Also, there is the matter of sand dribbling out of the trunk. Car trunks are airtight as a rule in order to keep whatever's in them dry in case of rain. Finally, it would seem next to impossible for the little girl to have ever found her way back to the beach, scooping up sand as she went from the highway.

Somewhat discouraged, I reread my notes. Then

I ask myself: Did Hansel and Gretel find their way back home the first night tracking stones? Did the wolf actually speak English to Red Riding Hood? Without Rapunzel's hair, how did the witch ever climb the tower to begin with? I sigh, and leave the story in my notes the way it is, EMBELLISHED.

Uncle Max's Story

My family history project may be about to take a turn for the better. I think Mother is starting to feel sorry for me. "Ashley," she says, having read my notes on the mandrake root and sandbox, "I really don't see what either story has to do with your project." I was afraid that she would say that. I'm more afraid she may be right.

"You don't understand," I tell her.

In any event, and whatever her reasons, Mother, it seems, has decided to be helpful. Lately, she has fallen into the habit of saying, anytime she speaks with a relative, "Ashley is doing a family history project for her social studies class. Have you any information that might help?" It makes no difference to her, either, whether the person is related by blood or marriage. That is how I came to hear Uncle Max's story in the first place.

Uncle Max is Alexandra's father. He stops by one evening after work to deliver a book to Mother from Aunt Elizabeth. Trading books is something they do often.

"It isn't actually my story," Uncle Max explains. "It happened to my sister's husband's mother. My sister recorded it on tape the year she went searching for her roots. She took a tape recorder with her nearly everywhere she went." Remembering, he sighs. "It was a trying time," he says.

"Roots?" Mother sounds interested. "Ashley knows a little story about some sort of root." She looks meaningfully at me. She's referring, of course, to my mandrake root. She's trying to be funny.

"Yes," says Uncle Max politely, and then continues with his story. It is something I find out as my project progresses: Most people are most interested in their own stories or stories almost like their own.

"When my sister made her tape," Uncle Max goes on, "her mother-in-law was in her eighties. The story took place at least half a century before. A story like that, a person couldn't forget.

"She had escaped from her town in Russia, she related, with a group of other women. Nearly all of them had children, many of them babies. They wandered for days, then weeks, finally months, across fields and borders, bribing guards with what little jewelry they possessed. It was winter and very cold. One night they stood at the edge of a forest in the middle of what seemed to them nowhere but was probably Poland. They saw faint lights in the distance, and they walked toward them. They came to a small town, only a village, a group of houses really and some barns. There was a synagogue. Jewish people lived there. Now they would be saved. At least they would not freeze—That's what they thought. Well," says Uncle Max, "you would have thought so, too, if you had been there with them.

"The women tried to enter the synagogue. The door was locked. They knocked, they pounded, they tried to push it open. Finally, somebody from inside unlocked it, opened it barely a crack. It was a man who asked them what they wanted. What could they have wanted except to be warm?

"My sister's mother-in-law said it was a rabbi at the door. She *thought* it was a rabbi. 'No,' the rabbi told the women. 'You can't come in,' he said, looking at the children. She was in her eighties when she said it. Maybe she was wrong. Maybe it was a night watchman at the door.

"Still, he wouldn't let them in. He told them he'd had experiences before, with women just like them. They'd mess up his synagogue. 'The children,' he said, 'would piss on the floor.'" Uncle Max looks carefully at Mother. "That is exactly what she said the rabbi had said, according to my sister.

"'Women like what?' my sister said angrily, relating the story to me, repeating the words of the rabbi, or watchman. 'Did he mean bad experiences with women and children fleeing from Russia, women who had seen husbands and children murdered, who had watched from hiding places, helpless, seeing them killed because they were Jewish? Were they the kind of women he meant?'

"Women like that, in any event," Uncle Max says, almost smiling, "do not readily take no for an answer. These were no exception. They pushed the man, rabbi or watchman, to one side and opened the door. They slept inside that night, and they were warm. They broke up the benches for firewood, and when they needed more, they took down a door. The children, according to my sister's mother-in-law, did, after all, piss on the floor. 'Was there anything else,' she asked my sister, 'that we could have done? You'd have done the same,' she said, 'if you'd been with us.'" Uncle Max leans back in his chair and sighs, finished with the story.

I thank him for telling it to me.

"I'm glad I could help," he answers. Before he leaves, he says to me, "Ash, could I ask you for a favor?" Oh, no, I think, but he surprises me.

"If you use that story in your project, please could you include her name, my sister's mother-in-law's name? It would seem a shame," he says, "to get the story right, but miss the name."

Now, I think, I'm getting somewhere. I give Mother what I intend as a meaningful look. If she notices, she does not show it. "Sure," I say. "What was her name?"

"Eva Feldman," Uncle Max replies. He writes it down and hands the paper to me. "Eva Feldman," he repeats. "I'll check the spelling with my sister. If I've spelled it wrong, I'll call you."

He has spelled it right and does not call. He does send me the tape, the one his sister made and saved in her attic. But the tape gets erased when Father tries to show me how to operate his tape recorder. I think then what a good thing it was I wrote the story down after I had heard it and saved my notes. "Always save your notes," I will tell my students should it ever turn out I teach social studies, though I doubt I will.

"Always make a copy of your tape," Uncle Max says the day I finally bring myself to tell him. Uncle Max, it turns out, made a copy of the tape before he mailed it. I feel as if a burden has been lifted from me when I hear it.

Hitting Harry on the Head

The week before my project notes are due, my cousin Alexandra comes to visit for the weekend. It is something that she does from time to time, or I go there. Alexandra is only three months older, but a year ahead of me in school.

Although our mothers are identical, Alexandra and I do not look alike, nor do we resemble them to any appreciable degree. For one thing, both of them are redheads. Any way they wear their hair—loose with little braids, pulled back in a bun, coiled in a chignon—it adds distinction to their looks. Not at all like ours, which is tree bark brown and crinkly and flies in every direction. "There must be something we can do with their hair," our mothers used to tell each other when we were small.

Beyond that, Alexandra is beautiful, while I am ordinary. "How can you say 'ordinary'?" Mother likes to argue. "You are exotic, just like a Kirghiz princess." It didn't mean a thing to me until last summer, when I read Russian novels deciding I'd much rather look American, whatever that might mean, and look like Alexandra, who is tall and slim with everything about her long—long legs, long arms, long nose and toes and fingers. About three-quarters of her height, I think, is leg. "You are so long-waisted, Ash," Mother has said to me on occasion, as though paying me a compliment. Long-waisted means short-legged. I am barely five feet three and sturdy. Father says I'm bound to grow at least another inch, and maybe two. He marks my progress on the closet door in pencil. I'd much rather be like Alexandra, angular.

I would also like to have her eyes, eyes which are not angular. They are large and round and gray. Mine are nearly black and slanted. "Lovely, almond-shaped," says Mother. Hers and Aunt Elizabeth's are green. At least I don't need glasses. "I need mine only for seeing," Alexandra jokes. Aunt Elizabeth will not allow her to get contact lenses. "Maybe when you're older," she has said, but not promised.

"Family history project," Alexandra says after I've explained, now that she's unpacked. Well, unpacking wasn't much. She opened up her zipper bag, held it upside down, and let its contents fall into the open dresser drawer my mother had emptied for her. "There," she said, "that's done," then looked around for a place to put her zipper bag, found an empty corner, and set it down there.

"I did a family history project last year," she informs me. "Everybody has to do one in tenth grade."

"Really?" I say. "I didn't know that." I picture mothers of tenth graders in every town and city in the state, running to libraries before schools let out, frantically checking out all the same books. I ask Alexandra hopefully, "Do you still have yours?"

"Are you kidding?" Alexandra responds. "Why would I have saved it? Especially," she adds, "in a family like ours. Besides, most of it I just made up."

"You might have saved it," I point out, "knowing I could use it this year." Of course, I do not mean use it only to copy from. I mean I could have used it as a reference source, one more entry in my bibliography.

"I'll tell you a story about me," Alexandra offers. "You can put that in your project."

"Some help that will be."

Alexandra regards me coolly. "If there is one thing I know about family history," she says, "it is that every member of the family counts. Had you done your research," she points out, "you'd know to start not necessarily with the person who knows the most, but with the one with whom you feel most comfortable. It could be a brother or sister."

"I don't have a brother or a sister."

"That," she says, "is what I'm trying to tell you. For an only child like you, the next best thing is a first cousin, like me. I will tell you about the worst experience in my life. Well, worst up to the time when it happened. I was five."

I get my pencil and some paper. I think we have nothing better to do at the moment; also, Alexandra can be very entertaining when she tries.

We sit on the floor, and Luther, the cat, sits in my lap, chewing my pencil eraser, while I try to take notes. Alexandra speaks theatrically, waving her hands in the air as we have always been told not to do, although to this day we both still put down packages before we speak.

"The day when I, Alexandra, threw my shovel in the air," she begins, "and it flew up and landed on top of Harry's head and made him bleed counted as the worst day in my life. Also Harry's. They took Harry to the hospital and got him stitches. Mother took me to my room and told me, 'Stay there!' She didn't say how long. Days, I thought; it could be weeks. I knew better than to ask.

"I did what I could to make myself comfortable. I pulled my wooden rocking chair over by the window, held my stuffed duck, Jessamyn, tightly in my lap, and covered both our heads with my blue-and-yellow baby blanket. I settled down to wait.

"I sat and waited. I rocked in my chair and petted Jessamyn. I did not chew my blanket. 'Only babies chew on blankets,' Mother used to say, as though I'd care. But when Father told me he would cut the blanket into smithereens if I didn't stop chewing on it, that was when I stopped."

I try to picture Uncle Max saying "smithereens."

"Afterward," continues Alexandra, "I started chewing on my thumb."

"Chewing on your thumb will make it short," we'd both been warned at one time or another by our mothers. "There's a man in your stomach," they told us, "the one who growls when he's hungry. When your thumb is in your mouth, he chews the end of it for food. See," they'd say, "it's getting short already."

We both had stopped believing the day when Alexandra pointed out to me that everybody's thumb was short. "Thumb means short finger," she explained to both of us. After that we stopped believing everything our mothers said.

"But still," says Alexandra, "right that minute in my room, the man was growling. I was ready to believe in anything. 'You,' I said to the man in my stomach. 'You down there, be still. You only think that you are hungry. Just wait until nighttime comes,' I warned. 'Harry may be dead for all we know, and they won't feed us anything in jail, not even bread.' Go to your room and stay there, was all the information that I had. Harry could have bled to death and no one told me.

"So I sat in my room with my duck, and I prayed. 'Please, God,' I prayed, 'don't let Harry die.' I wasn't sure whether they would put a five-year-old in jail or not. Probably not, I told myself. But then where would they put me? I had no idea. I could hear my mother pleading with the police who'd come to get me. 'Please,' she'd say. 'She's just a child. She's barely five, she just turned four, she's only three.'

"Actually what I heard was Mother speaking on the telephone to Father. I got up from my chair, tip-toed across the room, and listened with my ear against the door. I couldn't make out a word that she was saying. I tiptoed back and tried banging my head against the windowsill for a while, testing. It didn't hurt that much. 'That baby Harry,' I whispered to Jessamyn, 'had to go and make himself bleed. He probably only did it for attention.'"

It was something our mothers were forever telling us. "Stop whining," they'd say. "You know you only do it for attention." Sometimes they even told it to the other mothers, just in case the other mothers hadn't found out for themselves. "Oh," our mothers would inform them, "you know children, they'll do anything for attention."

"Couldn't they see, I thought at the time," says Alexandra, "that Harry was the one who would do anything to get attention? I wondered what was happening to him. I thought he'd probably need stitches.

"'I'm sure that he'll need stitches,' I had heard the other mothers say as I was being led away. 'Stitches,' I explained to Jessamyn, 'will sometimes leave a scar.'"

Those were the years when Alexandra and I were forever trying to get scars. "Don't pick at scabs," they always told us; "it will leave a scar." We, therefore, were forever picking. We picked at cuts and bruises, at mosquito bites, at scratches. "Maybe," we told each other, "it's just something grownups say to fool children." They were always saying something to see if they could trick us. "In a minute," they'd say, meaning "in a few hours"; "if you're good," they would say, meaning "probably not"; "we'll see," they said, when they meant "absolutely under no circumstances, never."

Luther yawns and rests his head against my knee. Alexandra stretches her feet in front of her, shoeless, and goes on with her story.

" 'Harry has a hole in his head, want to come see,' was what Jeremy, Harry's brother, had said to Scott, enticing him from the seesaw. Hole in his head, I thought to myself in my room, trying to imagine what it might be like, imagining a person with a hole could see inside his head. Of course he'd need a flashlight and two mirrors, one to look, the other to reflect. Well, having a dentist for a father, I knew about such things. If it were me, I thought, I'd look.

"I began to get hungry. It seemed as if I hadn't eaten anything for days. I could hear Mother in the kitchen making lunch, burning toast. I wondered if I cried would Mother hear me and be sorry. Maybe she would say like normal mothers, 'Would you like some lunch, Alexandra? A nice piece of buttered toast.' Probably not, I decided. It would only make her angrier. She was already angry enough for one day, I could tell. I took Jessamyn and climbed into bed for a nap. Remember how we hated naps,"

Alexandra reminds me. It was true. Both of us had always screamed against taking them.

"What can be wrong with them?" our mothers used to ask each other. "Normal children take naps. Don't you want to be like the other children?" they scolded.

"I thought if I were sleeping," says Alexandra, "I wouldn't know I was so hungry. It was true. I didn't know. In fact, when I woke up, it was already evening. Father was home. It was nearly dark outside. I heard them talking in the kitchen, talking louder coming down the hallway toward my room. I pulled the blanket over my head and pretended to be sleeping. I told myself that sleeping people don't get sent to jail. They wait for them to wake up first."

"I never wake up Alexandra when she's sleeping," Aunt Elizabeth used to say to Mother. "Even if the house were on fire, I think I would wait. She is a terrible child when she first wakes up. I do not understand," she'd say, bewildered, "a child who hates to nap but is so ugly getting up." Alexandra used to look in the mirror for ugly. Where ugly? she'd wonder. Did she mean ugly eyes, ugly nose, ugly what? "Alexandra's such a pretty child," everybody else was always saying. Even I always said it.

"Well," says Alexandra, "Father wasn't fooled. He bent over, picked me up, and kissed me. 'Tears,' he said, then, 'Salt.' I hadn't known that I was crying. 'I hear that you've had quite a day.'

" 'It was an accident,' I told him.

" 'Some accident,' said Mother."

I could hear her saying it. It is exactly what my mother would have said. A stranger only listening to them would know that they were twins. It isn't just what they say, either, but how. Even I, even Alexandra, cannot tell them apart on the telephone.

"Hello. Aunt Elizabeth? Is this Aunt Elizabeth? How are you?"

"Don't be silly," says the voice. "This is your mother."

You would think that they would hate it. Instead, they are delighted.

"It was really quite funny," Mother says. "I called Uncle Max at his office, and his nurse simply wouldn't believe I wasn't Elizabeth. She thought I was playing a joke." Smiling, Mother claps her hands together with pleasure.

"Father insisted," says Alexandra, "that I tell him the entire story from the start. 'Tell me exactly what happened,' he said. So I did.

" 'I was mad,' I told him, although even then I couldn't remember why.

" 'Angry, Alexandra,' Mother interrupted. 'Dogs get mad. People just get angry.'

" 'I was so mad,' I continued, 'that I threw my shovel in the air. It accidentally fell on Harry.'

" 'Requiring eleven stitches in his head,' Mother interjected.

"Stitches in his head, I thought; surely it meant he wasn't dead. 'I'm so glad,' I whispered, 'Harry didn't die.'

" 'Die,' said Father. 'Why would you have thought he died?'

" 'So much blood,' I said cautiously. 'He screamed so loudly. Probably,' I said, feeling enormously relieved, feeling safe for the first time that day since it happened, 'he only did it for attention.'

" 'I don't think so, Alexandra,' said my father. Then he said, 'Go wash your hands and face. We're going to see Harry.'

" 'If it's all the same,' I said, 'I'd just as soon stay home.'

" 'It isn't all the same,' said Father. 'Your mother and I are going with you. You're going to apologize.' I washed my hands and face.

"When we arrived at Harry's house, Harry still looked pale. He had a bandage on his head, but I could see around its edges where they'd shaved his hair away. He was sitting on the sofa with his mother.

" 'I'm sorry,' I told him, 'that my shovel hit you in the head. I didn't mean it to. I shouldn't have thrown it in the air. You can have my shovel, Harry. I don't want it anymore.' Actually," says Alexandra, "I hadn't the faintest idea where my shovel had gone to after landing on Harry.

" 'That's okay,' said Harry, moving closer to his mother.

"Harry's mother said, 'I'm sure that Alexandra's learned her lesson and that everyone has had enough excitement for one day.' She stood, ready to usher us out. I moved toward the door. 'Tomorrow we'd be glad for Alexandra to come back and visit.'

"I hoped her saying so was just another way to be polite and that I wouldn't have to do it. 'That would be nice,' I answered politely.

"As it turned out," Alexandra tells me, "I didn't have a choice. 'I hope,' Mother said, as she kissed me good night, 'you really did learn a lesson.'

" 'Oh, yes,' I assured her cheerfully.

" 'That's good,' she said. 'Because you know, learning one's lesson is nice, but making amends is also important.' I did not have to know what 'amends' meant to understand I would not care for them.

"Harry's mother, as it happened, needed assistance digging in her garden. 'I've arranged,' Mother informed me, 'for you to go and help her first thing after breakfast. You can borrow Harry's shovel.'

"I wondered for how long I'd have to help. Suppose they made me shovel all the way to China."

Both our mothers spent years of their childhood, or so they have told us, digging in the dirt, trying to reach China. "Are you sure?" they used to ask our grandmother. "Are you sure we can get to China this way?"

"Sure," she answered. "You just have to keep digging." Children, she informed the other mothers, will believe anything you tell them.

"Well," says Alexandra, "I thought China would have to be better than jail; roast duck and Chinese tea better than dry bread and water, which Grandma used to warn me was all a prisoner got." Alexandra stops talking.

"Is that it?" I ask.

"Isn't it enough? Believe me, it was more than enough at the time."

I believe her, but still I want to know what happened the next morning.

"In the morning," she says, "I shoveled, what else?"

"And," I say.

"And what?"

"Did Harry, or didn't Harry, have a scar?"

"You know," she says, "I never did find out. I tried to make him show me, but he wouldn't. Then, by the time his bandages came off, his hair had pretty much grown back, and I could never tell. But it always seemed to me he must have. Probably he has it still. Probably he tells his friends he got it in a fight. I bet he never says it came when he was four from being hit in the head with a shovel by a girl."

I thank Alexandra for her story. I think it will go well with my sandbox tale. Projects should be organized, Ms. Baxter often tells us. Logical order, relevant progression, she says, are important. Relevant or not, I can't be certain, but I feel I'm making progress.

"Tomorrow," Alexandra promises, "I'll help some more."

Interviews and Telephone Calls

Tomorrow, Saturday, before we're even up, Sylvia is knocking on my bedroom door. She has come to trade her social studies book with me.

"Your mom let me in," she explains. "I'm in a hurry. I promised Eddie I would take him to the zoo to see the penguins." Eddie is her younger brother. He is seven. He plans to be an ornithologist when he grows up. "Eddie was born middle-aged," I have heard their mother say.

Sylvia's book is yellow. It is called *Country Folks:*

A Handbook for Student Folklore Collectors and contains a section on "Family History."

"I was really lucky," she explains, "to get this book. It was in the wrong place on the shelf. Otherwise, it would have been checked out before I ever got there, just like all the others."

The book she borrows from me in exchange is the one from which my sandbox story came. I do not lend her the one with the mandrake root, not because I am the sort of person who wants to get ahead no matter how, but because I know it will be of no use to her whatsoever. Also, I do not care to give it up just yet.

"So long," Sylvia says, popping out of my room the way she popped in. "I have to run."

I step over Alexandra, who is sleeping on the floor, although I have an extra bed. "A guest bed will be nice," Mother said when she bought it. "You can have friends over to sleep in it." But friends never do. Either, like Alexandra, they prefer my floor, or they share my bed, or they bring sleeping bags with them when they come. "The floor is better for my back," Alexandra explains, sitting up.

Together we do exercises, six stretches, eight touch our toes, and three swamis to the east which I learned in yoga. I go into the bathroom to brush my teeth and wash my face.

When I return, Alexandra is sitting cross-legged on my bed, cassette recorder next to her, reading the yellow book. "Our day's work is cut out for us," she informs me. "Step by step, it tells you here exactly how to do your project." One thing I will say for Alexandra, if a book's at hand, she'll read it.

"The first thing we'll do," she says, "is interview for anecdotes. We'll start with you."

"Why me?"

"Because 'you are as much a bearer of your family's traditions as any member of your family,'" she reads out loud. She turns on the tape recorder. I can think of nothing interesting to say.

"My life is not *that* interesting," I tell her.

"Don't worry," she answers. "I'll read you questions from the book to jog your mind. Relax and concentrate. 'Think of any proverbs you may know, or sayings about the weather. Do you know jump rope rhymes, or ghost stories?'" She pauses. I sigh. Undiscouraged, she reads on. "'Have you ever cooked something following your mother's recipe?'"

I think of kasha. "I have cooked kasha," I say.

"Kasha," she says into the recorder, "is a kind of cereal, a buckwheat grown in Eastern Europe. It is important," she tells me, "to explain the context of a story and any foreign words." I do not think that "kasha" is a foreign word. It is sold in the supermarket, after all. I don't stop to point this out.

"There is no way," I point out instead, "to cook a little kasha, less than a roomful, for instance. I know because I've tried. 'It's enough to feed an army,' Mother said last time, then added, 'Remember when you were little and I used to read to you the story of the magic cooking pot? It was Italian.'

" 'An Italian pot?' I asked.

" 'An Italian story,' Mother said, recalling it for me.

" 'There was a wizard once,' she said, 'who owned a magic cooking pot. One day the wizard hired an apprentice to help in the kitchen, but not to learn the secret of the pot. A secret learned is, after all, no secret. But the apprentice listened anyway, his ear to the keyhole, and learned the magic words to start the pot. He did not, however, learn the words to make it stop.

" 'It happened not too many days after that the wizard went away, out of town on business. Naturally the apprentice could not wait. Right away he started cooking pasta in the pot. Of course, he couldn't make it stop. Soon pasta filled the pot, the room, the house, almost the entire village.'

" 'Almost just like Ashley's kasha,' my father said, interrupting Mother's story, as she hates him to do.

" 'Almost, but not quite,' she answered. 'In any event, when the wizard finally did return, her business done, there was pasta everywhere. She whispered the magic words to stop the pot, fired her apprentice, and fed the town spaghetti every day all year.'

" 'That's an interesting story. It's just like one my mother used to tell me.' Father paused to eat some of my kasha.

" 'Exactly just like it or a little just like it?' Mother asked.

" 'Well, there was a pot in the story,' Father said, 'but it was a Russian pot. And it was a little girl who did the cooking in place of an apprentice, and what got cooked was porridge instead of pasta.'

" 'I see,' Mother said. 'But there was a magic word to start the pot, isn't that so?'

" 'Not magic,' said Father. 'The mother would just say, "Little pot, cook porridge." Only, of course,' he explained, 'she said it in Russian. And when she wanted it to stop, she'd only have to say, "Stop pot," also in Russian. But,' he said, 'although the little girl was in the kitchen when the porridge started, she always had to go wash her hands before she ate. Therefore, she was never there to hear her mother say, "Stop pot."

" 'It happened one day that the mother had to be

away, and the little girl got hungry. She thought, I'll just make myself some porridge to eat, and she did. But of course, she didn't know how to stop the pot, so by the time her mother got home there was porridge everywhere. It filled the pot, the kitchen, the cottage, and had even begun to drift into the woods.'

" 'Did she fire the little girl?' I asked.

" 'Of course not,' said Father. 'When the mother saw what had happened, she only said, "Stop pot," in Russian, naturally, and the little girl heard her say it, and after that she, too, could stop the pot. Only she didn't have to for a long time after."

" 'Why was that?' Mother asked.

" 'Because,' Father explained, 'they ate so much porridge the rest of that year it turned them against it for some time to come.' "

I turn off Alexandra's tape recorder. Alexandra laughs. "How *do* you say, 'Stop pot,' in Russian?" she asks.

"I don't know. I asked my father, but he said his mother never told him."

Just at that moment Mother calls us to come in for breakfast. It is oatmeal, oatmeal with raisins. I can't remember the last time Mother made oatmeal.

"How did you happen to make oatmeal this morning?" I ask.

Mother shrugs. "It just came to me. It seemed a good idea."

"Oatmeal always reminds me," says Father, "of a story my mother used to tell about a magic porridge pot."

"I know," I say, "but right this minute we haven't time to hear it. Alexandra and I are doing interviews for my social studies project. Can we call Grandma after breakfast?" Grandma lives in Florida.

"Florida is long distance," Mother points out, as if otherwise I might not know it.

"We'll just ask her one short thing," I promise.

Mother sighs. "Go ahead, call, but don't stay on all day. Don't forget to send my love," she adds.

"They're exactly alike," Alexandra says while I dial. She means, of course, her mother and mine.

When Grandma answers, Alexandra takes the receiver to explain to her about my project. She is flipping through the pages of the yellow book as she does so, looking for a question that will be appropriate to ask and brief to answer.

"So," Grandma says loudly enough for me to hear also, "if it's Ashley's project, what are you doing calling me?"

"I'm helping," Alexandra says.

"Some helping," says Grandma. "You should do

your own project and let Ashley do hers. It would be better helping."

"I am doing it," I say, taking the receiver from Alexandra. I read from the place in the yellow book where she points her finger.

"How did you pick the day on which you got married?" I ask. "The day you and Grandpa got married."

"That's it?" she asks. "That's what you called long distance from New York to ask? Your mother knows you're doing this? How did we pick the day? We picked the day because it was a holiday. That was how we picked it."

"Abraham Lincoln's birthday," I point out, "is not such a big holiday."

"Who said big? Did I say big? That was the point. It was big enough we didn't have to go to work. It was small enough that we could find a judge who'd marry us. Courtrooms aren't open weekends. When else did we have time?"

"That's it?" I ask. "That was your only reason?"

"That's it," she answers.

I thank her and tell her I'll be sure to include her story in my project. Then we say good-bye.

"That was interesting," says Alexandra, hanging up the phone.

"What was so interesting?" I ask. It didn't interest me. Then I recall that Aunt Elizabeth and Uncle Max got married on Christmas Day, in a synagogue, not a courtroom, by a rabbi, not a judge. "Max always wanted something he could celebrate on Christmas Day, when everybody else did," I have overheard my mother say. Now *that* I find is interesting. But when I tell her so, Alexandra only shrugs. "All they do is cook each other dinner. As celebrations go," she says, "it isn't much. I mean, it's nothing like a Christmas tree."

Next, we decide to call Grandpa Rush. He also lives in Florida, but in a different part. "Florida is bigger than Miami," he likes to say, meaning where Grandma Hofstaedter lives. Actually she lives in West Palm Beach, nearly seventy miles away. Grandpa insists it's all the same. "It's the place where Brooklyn moved," he says. Grandpa lives in Pensacola, on the Gulf side, a portion of the state that's called the panhandle.

"I guess it makes me a panhandler," he jokes.

"He means a pioneer," Father insists.

"I should have bought stock in the phone company," Mother says when we tell her our plans about calling.

"Hello, Grandpa," I say. "It's good to hear your

voice." My mother always says that: "It's good to hear your voice." I am surprised to hear me say it, surprised how much I sound like her, surprised I do not stop and start again.

"I'm doing a family history project, Grandpa," I explain. "I need an anecdote, something short from your childhood."

He thinks for a minute.

"It has to be short?" he asks.

I tell him yes. "Also, it's long distance," I remind him. "If you think of something long, maybe you will write it to me in a letter."

"Maybe. I remember only one short thing," he tells me.

"Good. Just wait until I get my tape recorder set."

"You're going to record my one short thing? I tell you, it's so short I don't think you'll forget it."

"Some of our interviews are supposed to be on tape," I explain, wondering now, too late, why I hadn't taped Grandma's conversation.

"Probably she wouldn't have let you," Alexandra points out later. "Probably it would have been an infringement of some rights." Probably Alexandra is correct.

Grandpa begins. "When I was a boy, pretty

small, maybe six years old, I flew." That is all he says. There is silence on the line.

"Is that it, Grandpa?" I ask. "You flew, that's the whole story?"

"You told me to tell something short. It's as short as I could get."

"Maybe," I suggest, "you could make it just a little longer. Maybe you could say what it was like when you flew."

"Wonderful," he says. "It was wonderful. I put out my arms, and I flapped very hard, and I flew. Maybe six feet off the ground, maybe more. It's a long time to remember."

"You mean," I say, realizing belatedly there were no planes when he was six, "you thought you flew."

"I actually did it," says Grandpa. "That's what my mother, your great-grandmother, said to me at the time: 'You mean you thought you flew.' Naturally she said it in Russian. Well, I was not about to contradict my mother. Also, as hard as I could, try as I did, all through the years, I've never been able to do it again. Still, there was that one time. So," he says, "you don't believe it. Who cares what you believe? What I want to know is why you call long distance to find out what you won't believe. Long distance is expensive, Ashley. Say hello to your parents for me." He hangs up the telephone.

Alexandra is watching me carefully. She is not thinking what I'm thinking. He is not her grandfather after all. She does not know him as I do. She cannot know that right this minute Grandpa isn't angry. He is only in a hurry. He has probably hurried off the phone to run outside to flap his arms to try just one more time to fly.

"Don't be silly, Ashley," Mother says when I tell her. "Grandpa was only teasing you."

"Maybe he was teasing her," my father says. "But I would not discount entirely the story of a man who carried all those sacks of kopeks on his back coming on a boat from Russia."

"I thought that they were pennies," Mother says.

"Kopeks, pennies, what's the difference?" says Father.

The last phone call we make is not long distance.

"I'm not *that* good at stories," Aunt Elizabeth informs us. Then, for a few moments, she doesn't say anything. Finally, she says, "You might be interested in knowing why there are no locks on any inside doors in any house where Grandma Hofstaedter lives."

I think about it for a minute. It is true, there are none. Even her bathroom doors don't lock. I always thought she did it to discourage dawdling. "Not even on the bathroom doors," I say into the phone.

"Especially not on the bathroom doors," Aunt Elizabeth replies. "The first thing Grandma does when she moves into any place is to take off all the locks. Your mother is the reason."

"My mother?"

"Your mother was always getting herself locked up, stuck, in places that she couldn't escape from. Accidentally, of course, but it was still hard to explain. It was also hard for your grandmother to extricate her. Sometimes she could, and sometimes she couldn't. One time Grandma got stuck halfway in and halfway out the bathroom window, trying. The fire department had to come rescue her. Then they took down the door and got Sonya out. Oh, was your grandmother ever angry. After that she decided it was simpler just to remove the locks, all the locks, all the time. It got to be a habit. She kept on doing it, even after we'd grown up, after we had moved away."

"Was that time the last time?" I ask, meaning the last time my mother ever got stuck anyplace.

"Oh, no," Aunt Elizabeth says. "Even without doors that locked, your mother found ways. The worst time was when she stuck her head through the back of a wooden dining-room chair, then couldn't get it out. 'They're very expensive chairs,' your grandmother kept saying, as if it mattered. We thought at the time, or anyway I did, that she might have to walk around for the rest of her life with a chair on her neck. Grandma tried oiling her neck. When that didn't work, your grandfather called the superintendent of the apartment building where we lived. He came with a saw and sawed out the back of the chair. I cried the whole time he was sawing. I was so afraid his saw would slip, and he'd cut off her head, and I would wind up as an only child. In those days," Aunt Elizabeth says, "we were taught to believe it was a terrible thing to be an only child. Thank goodness now it's changed." She means, thank goodness on account of Alexandra and me being only children.

"After that," Aunt Elizabeth concludes, "your grandfather borrowed the saw and cut out the backs of all the chairs in the rest of the set. 'They look better all the same,' he said. But I always thought he did it for the same reason Grandma took off locks."

"It's a good day's work, Ashley," Alexandra says as we hang up the phone.

Later Mother looks over my notes and reads that

story. "That's funny," she tells us, "I don't remember it that way at all. It wasn't me; it was Elizabeth who was always getting stuck. She is the reason Grandma always takes off locks."

"Are you sure?" Alexandra asks. "Are you absolutely certain? Mother seemed quite positive about its being you."

"Don't be silly," my mother answers. "Of course, I'm certain. To this day I still can see the way she looked with her head stuck through the bars. I remember it as if it happened yesterday, how afraid I was the saw would slip and I would be an only child. We had such bad opinions in those days of only children. Of course, we know now we were wrong," she adds apologetically.

"I sometimes think," Alexandra says later, "that being twins may not be all that it's cracked up to be."

It seems to me she may be right. Being an only child has some advantages.

CHAPTER 8

The Dancing Bear and Chimpanzee

Sunday evening, after dinner, Alexandra engages Father in a conversation. She encourages him to talk about his childhood. Well, Father doesn't need too much encouragement.

"Uncle Martin," says Alexandra, "tell us what life was like when you were our age."

"To tell the truth," says Father, addressing Alexandra, who hasn't seemed to notice Mother's warning look, "it was hard to know what went on then. Everything was secret. 'It's none of your business,' we were always being told by grownups. Things were so secret," he says, "that when my cousin Esther was born, it came as a complete surprise to Samuel. Samuel is Esther's brother. He was ten years old at the time." Alexandra appears to think it over.

"But he must have noticed something," she insists. "I mean, it had to have crossed his mind at least one time to wonder when he saw his mother getting big."

Father smiles at Alexandra kindly. "Believe me, in those days children didn't notice and they didn't wonder. And if they had, they wouldn't have been allowed. The way Samuel found out," Father explains, "was that Samuel's father sent Samuel to the neighbor's house with a note. It was a birth announcement: 'Tanya had a girl.' 'Congratulations,' the neighbor told Samuel, and that was when he knew. Well, he was so excited he ran all the way home to tell his father, who was my Uncle Yossel. 'Yes,' said his father, 'I know.' 'Congratulations,' they said to each other, 'isn't it wonderful?' Well, at least Samuel didn't say, 'Wait until Mother finds out. Won't she be pleased to hear such good news?'"

My own mother gives Father one of her famous looks. As usual, it could mean anything.

"Ashley's grandfather could really tell you some things," Father tells Alexandra. "It's too bad he isn't here with us today."

"Yesterday he told us that he flew," Alexandra informs Father. "Not in a plane." She flaps her elbows up and down by way of demonstrating how.

"So I've heard." Father doesn't bat an eye. "I wouldn't put it past him. When I was your age, he used to tell me stories about a chimpanzee in Russia, a white chimpanzee."

Mother pours herself a cup of coffee. "I didn't know," she says slowly, "there were chimpanzees in Russia, much less white ones."

Father shrugs. "Not chimpanzees," he says, emphasis on the plural. "Just one chimpanzee. Anyway, it's what he told me. I was not about to argue with my father."

"Do you remember the stories?" Alexandra asks. "Could you tell one?"

"Maybe," says Father. "I think maybe one. If I remember right, there was a bear in it, a dancing bear. Bears were popular in Russia. 'Oh, yes,' my father used to tell me, 'there were bears everywhere, in carnivals and circuses and sometimes standing on street corners.' Well, the bears on corners would have ropes around their necks or rings through their noses, and they'd shuffle in a circle, standing on their hind legs, and do a sort of two-step bear dance. At least most of them did. The men who owned the bears and held the ropes would sometimes be musicians. Then they'd blow into a mouth organ, or turn a hand one, or strum an instrument with strings, the balalaika, and the bears would dance in time to the music, or the other way around. Often the bears would be dressed in costumes that included hats. The hats would be tipped for people to put coins into. If the bear didn't wear a hat, usually the man did, and for the same purpose.

"Naturally my father was not supposed to waste the few coins he possessed by giving them to bears. Nor, of course, was his sister, Fanny. 'Still,' he used to tell me, 'some of those bears could be hard to resist.'"

"I thought this was a story about a chimpanzee," says Alexandra.

"It is," my father answers. "I'm coming to that part." Mother and I exchange looks.

"As I was saying," says Father, "there was a bear that stood on a corner in my father's village, not far from where he lived with his parents and his sister. This bear was not like the other bears. It was a very small bear for one thing, probably a baby, and very sad. It was always dressed in the same red jacket and no hat. It didn't dance very well either, not even as bears go. It didn't seem to know any steps. It would just sort of hobble about awkwardly on its two hind legs, trying its best to please. Sometimes it fell down. It always looked, according to my father, as if any minute it might start to cry. I think probably it missed its mother."

"Probably," says Mother, "it was a midget dressed up as a bear. Did you ever think of that?"

"Probably," I say, "it didn't want to be there in the first place."

"Probably," says Alexandra, "every dancing bear would rather be some other place in place of dancing."

"Please," says Father, "can I just go on with my story? Every day, as I was about to say, my father would walk by that bear as it stood on that same street corner, the rope around its neck, trying to two-step. Sometimes he would bring it food to eat, food he had to sneak from his mother's kitchen. He would wait until the man who held the rope was looking the other way before he fed the bear. According to my father, the man looked very mean. He had no hat and played no music, not even a mouth organ. He never smiled. He would just stand there and yank on the rope and wait for people to hand him coins, and they sometimes did, feeling sorry for the bear. Then he would stuff the coins into his pocket. My father was afraid of him.

"Nevertheless, one day he worked up sufficient courage to ask the man if he would sell him the bear. Apparently Father had it in mind somehow to buy the bear, then set him free. Where he would get the money from or what the bear would do once free, he hadn't figured out. Not that it mattered. The man wasn't planning to part with his bear.

" 'It's my living,' he told my father in a mean voice, then fleered at the bear.

"My father offered to hold the bear's rope for a while. 'Then you could go get something to eat,' he said to the man.

" 'I could do that now,' the man replied. 'The bear could go with me.' And saying that, my father said, the man tugged on the end of that poor bear's rope, and the bear looked sadder than ever."

This time Mother interrupts to ask, "Please, what about the chimpanzee?"

"I am just at that part," says Father. "It happened that in the village where my father lived, sometimes there was a zoo. Not much of a zoo as zoos go, just some animals in cages. People would pay a few coins to come look at them. It was a traveling zoo. It would stay a few months in one town, then move on to the next, and so on, until once every year, usually late in the fall, it would reappear outside my father's village.

"Well, this particular year, when the zoo came, it included for the first time a white chimpanzee, very rare, probably an albino." Father looks at Mother, who doesn't say a word. "As you can imagine," he points out, "it was the main attraction. It was not a very pleasant animal. It would watch the people watching it and make faces at them. It scratched itself in awkward places. It made rude noises and still ruder gestures, although about the latter my father never gave details. Then, one day, a villager came too near its cage and upset the chimpanzee. It grabbed onto the bars, enraged, and screeched, then beat its chest with its own fists, and last of all, it sprayed the man."

"Sprayed the man with what?" I ask.

Alexandra kicks me under the table. "Peed on the man, he means," she whispers.

Mother shakes her head. She disapproves of slang no matter what the circumstances. "Urinated," she automatically corrects. She is, after all, a scientist.

Father looks embarrassed. "In any event," he continues hurriedly, "you can imagine how the people watching laughed. That poor man shook his fist, first at the chimpanzee, then at the people. 'Just you wait,' he shouted, 'see if I don't get even.'

"That was why when the chimpanzee disappeared a few days later, a lot of people, including my father, thought first of that man. The zookeeper thought of him, too, but he didn't have any proof. He offered a reward but never had to pay it. No one found the chimpanzee. It did start my father thinking, however. If a chimpanzee could be freed, why not a bear? And as he told himself, for all he knew, it could have been a stolen bear to start with.

" 'Where'd you get the bear from?' my father asked the man.

" 'What's it to you?' the man answered.

" 'Just making conversation. I'm interested in bears.'

" 'Then go read a bear book. Beat it,' the man told him.

"That night my father talked it over with his sister, Fanny.

" 'If we get caught, it's stealing,' she told him. Well," Father points out, "it would be stealing either way. Logic was never Fanny's strong point. Still, my father insisted it wouldn't be stealing if the bear had been kidnapped in the first place. On his side was the fact that the bearman didn't act at all like other bearmen, and of course, the bear couldn't dance. 'Not your ordinary act,' Father said.

" 'But we don't know for certain,' Fanny insisted.

"The upshot was she agreed to stand guard while Father grabbed the bear. Fanny saw all of life as relative. If she didn't actually have to touch the bear, she told herself, whatever she did would not be stealing.

"That same night, when everybody else was sleeping, the two of them left home and walked to the edge of the town, where the bearman made his home in an abandoned barn. He was sound asleep, the bear's rope tied around one leg. The bear, hearing the children, grunted. The man, hearing the bear, turned over in his sleep. 'Sssh,' the children warned the bear. Then my father opened his knife to cut the rope. Just as he did, he and Fanny heard a rattling, chattering sound. It was the chimpanzee, which had also made its way to the abandoned barn and was hiding out there. Fanny and my father were not pleased to know it.

"The chimpanzee, however, seemed content to stay where it was high in the rafters, making little noises now and then, watching as my father sawed on the rope with his knife. Either the rope was thicker than he'd thought, or his knife was duller than he'd hoped, but it was taking much longer than he'd planned. Finally, though, the rope was cut through, and the bear was free. It didn't seem to know it.

"'Come on, bear,' Fanny whispered to it.

"'Come on, bear,' said Father, and he tugged at the cut end of its rope.

It was just at that moment the man woke up. Then he stood up. It was also just at that moment the chimpanzee let out a screech, surely loud enough to be heard in the center of the village, then leaped from where he had crouched seconds before on the rafters, and landed smack on the bearman's chest. The bearman was knocked back onto the floor and lay there motionless. Whether he was stunned by fright or by the impact, Father and Fanny could never be sure.

"'At least he's not dead,' Father said, seeing the bearman's chest move up and down as he breathed. He tugged one more time on the rope. This time the bear stood up, but instead of following Father, he knocked the rope from his hand and followed the white chimpanzee from the barn. Together they walked in the opposite direction of the village. Father and Fanny didn't stay to watch them. They ran as fast as they could all the way home and never stopped once until they were safe in their beds. 'Sssh,' Fanny said. 'Ssssh,' Father agreed. And so long as they lived in Russia, they never told a soul.

"The next morning the bearman came to town as usual, naturally without his bear. He shook his head and muttered to himself. 'I was lying there asleep,' he said, 'when suddenly a chimpanzee attacked me and took away my bear. The chimpanzee was white,' he added. Of course, no one believed him. Not even the zookeeper.

" 'You mean my chimpanzee was in your arms, and you just let it walk away. What kind of animal trainer are you anyway?' he jeered.

" 'A bearkeeper,' said the man. 'I'm a bearkeeper, not a trainer.'

" 'That much at least was true,' my father said. 'He'd never even taught his bear to dance.' Peasants passing through the village later on that year, however, sometimes told, amazed, of having seen in the countryside a chimpanzee and bear. 'The chimpanzee was white,' they'd say, 'and that bear was some dancer.'

" 'You've had too much to drink,' the villagers would say, 'or maybe you were dreaming.' "

"Well, of course, they were," says Mother. "That bear could never dance."

"Not on a rope," says Father, "but free, I bet he learned in no time."

"What difference does it make?" asks Alexandra. "It's just a made-up story."

"Who said 'made-up'?" asks Father. "I never said it was made up. My father used to tell it to me. If he had made it up, it would have had a moral. All the stories he made up had morals."

Alexandra doesn't say a word. Nor do I. I only picture in my head Grandpa flying here from Russia, his sister Fanny at his side. Both of them, I think, were probably in some hurry.

CHAPTER 9

Aunt Elizabeth Pays a Visit

W hen I arrive home from school the Friday after Alexandra's visit, Aunt Elizabeth is in our living room, curled up on our sofa like a cat. She is reading. Aunt Elizabeth can curl up anywhere and be at home. It is a talent that I envy. I hear Mother in the kitchen.

"Hi, Aunt Elizabeth," I say.

"Hi, Ash," she answers.

"I'm going to my room to put away my things. I'll be right back." Their voices may fool me on the telephone, but in person I would never mix them up.

"When we were children, you wouldn't have been able to tell us apart then," Mother insists. "Even Grandma had trouble. She used to write our names in crayon on the bottoms of our shoes."

"When you were our age," Alexandra and I once asked, "did you dress alike?"

"Why would we have done that?" Our question seemed to mystify them.

"Because of being twins," we pointed out. "Lots of twins dress alike."

"Oh," they said, "we weren't that kind of twins. And had we been," they added, "your grandmother wouldn't have heard of it." Grandma, it is true, has strong opinions about dress.

"Come here," she once said to Alexandra. "What do you call what you have on?"

"Shorts," said Alexandra.

"Umm," she said. "Don't you think they're rather short?"

"They're running shorts," Alexandra explained.

"I see," Grandma said, "but we're not running anyplace this minute, are we?"

"Not this minute," Alexandra agreed.

"You know," Grandma pointed out, "if you wear running shorts when you're not running, or in this case, even when you are, people might get the wrong impression of why you are wearing them. Exactly why," she asked, "are you wearing them?"

"I think I'll go change," said Alexandra.

"That's a good idea," Grandma agreed.

"Why can't you act normal, at least while your grandmother's here?" Aunt Elizabeth hissed as Alexandra headed for her bedroom.

It happens that our mothers dress alike now, but they don't seem to know it, and neither I nor Alexandra has ever had the heart to tell them. I do not mean they dress alike in the exact same dress or both in navy blue on the same day. I mean, they dress alike in general. Their closets are filled with clothes in the same bright colors and similar styles. Except for Mother's laboratory uniform, neither of them favors trousers, although Mother will put on my old jeans for jogging, and Aunt Elizabeth, who never exercises that I know of, occasionally will lounge in warm-ups of velour. They both buy skirts that wrap around; they wear a lot of scarves. I have discussed the matter of their clothes with Alexandra.

"Our mothers don't get dressed," I once apprised her, "as normal people do. They get wrapped up."

It was not news to her. "It's only natural," she informed me. "If you were a twin, you would, too. They do it for security. It's hard enough being single to know where one begins and ends. For a twin, it is impossible." Alexandra, it turned out, was studying psychology.

I go back to the living room to visit with my aunt. It happens several times a year that she and Mother take vacation days from work to spend them with each other. Aunt Elizabeth works in Bloomingdale's; she also writes a column for her local newspaper. Writing, she likes to explain, is her real work. Bloomingdale's is just for earning money.

"So, Ashley," Aunt Elizabeth says in Mother's voice, looking up from her book, "how is your project coming?"

"Fine," I lie, "it's almost finished." It is uncanny how alike they sound. I am not certain, though, it comes from being twins. They also sound a lot like Grandma Hofstaedter.

"Why should it bother me," I asked Alexandra, "that they all speak the same?"

"Because it isn't natural, that's why," Alexandra explained.

"Grandma talks funny," I used to complain.

"Talks funny how?"

" 'Hellome,' she says into the telephone when answering. 'Hellome,' and then she speaks. Why doesn't she say 'hello,' like everybody else?"

"Oh," Mother said, "I never noticed."

Well, of course she never noticed. Mother's speech is equally embarrassing.

"Your mother has an accent," the other children used to say. "Where is she from?"

"From? She's from around here," I'd mumble into my hand.

"What did you say? From where? Speak louder, we can't hear you."

"She's from around here," I'd say again, positive this time I was shouting. "Don't shout," I was forever being told by one or the other of my parents. "Modulate your tones," they would intone. "She's from around here," I'd say again, softer.

Before I started school, I used to think that there were grownups who could speak without making any sound, just by moving their lips, and that there were other grownups who understood them when they did it. It probably came from living in a home where everybody spoke in modulated tones. One day a lady in a purple dress on an elevator said to me softly, "Little girl, you are wrinkling up your nose. Unless you are a rabbit, you shouldn't be doing that." I was getting over a cold at the time. Well, grownups will say almost anything to children, that much I already knew. So *what* she said did not especially surprise me. It did surprise me, though, to realize she had only mouthed it and I had understood. I shared the news with Alexandra.

"Don't be silly," she told me. "There are some things even grownups will not say out loud to children. You heard whispering."

What I hear now is Aunt Elizabeth speaking to me.

"Pardon me. What did you say?"

"I asked you," she repeats patiently, "if you included the story about your mother's dog in your project."

"Dog? I didn't know you had a dog." Mother has told me on numerous occasions that they were not allowed to have pets.

"I," Aunt Elizabeth says pointedly, "did not have a dog. It was your mother's dog entirely. Never get a Doberman, I will tell you that. They're crazy. 'High-strung' the dogman called it, the one we finally got to come take the dog away. But even before that dog your mother had pets. She was always good at finding some furry creature or another to carry home and hide. I was always getting blamed. 'Do you hear something mewing, squeaking, barking?' our mother was forever asking me. 'No, do you?' I'd answer, looking out for Sonya. Why I've never known. She blamed me, too.

" 'Why can't you beg for a dog, whine for a cat, the way I do?' she'd yell. 'They'd let you have one.

They'd let you have anything, except you never ask.'
She'd pinch me as she spoke. 'You know you want
one, too.' Actually I didn't. I was afraid of dogs and
cats. I could never bring myself to tell your mother
that." This is a side to their relationship I have not
heard before.

"Pinching," my mother says later when I mention it. "Elizabeth was the one who always pinched.
Grandma never saw her do it. Once in a while, hardly
ever, I would hit her back. Grandma always saw that.
'Sonya, go to your room,' she would say. I spent
years of my childhood alone in my room."

"The point about the dog," says Aunt Elizabeth,
"is that it would bite anything that moved, and even
if a person were only standing still, apparently for
practice it would sometimes take a nip. It seemed to
think it was protecting Sonya. It protected her
twenty-four hours a day. When she was away, it
would turn its attention to protecting her posses-
sions, which it seemed to think included the entire
room we shared and everything in it. Thank goodness she had the dog only for one summer, at the end
of which none of our neighbors were speaking to us,
and several were suing. It came in handy that year
that our mother was a lawyer."

"What happened to the dog?" I ask.

"Well, even purebred with papers, finding

someone to take him, take him *and* keep him, wasn't
that easy. Selling him wasn't even a consideration.
Several people took him, but until the dogman came,
each one brought him back. 'He'll do fine for breed-
ing,' said the dogman, hauling him away. Anytime I
see a Doberman," says Aunt Elizabeth, "champing at
its leash, I wonder if it could be one of Sonya's dog's
descendants."

"Speaking of pets," Mother says, coming in, as
she so often does, on the tail end of the conversation,
"our grandmother from Poland had a parrot. She
called it a polly. One time she painted its cage, and it
ate off the paint, and it died."

"And?" I say.

"And nothing. I just happened to remember."

I sigh, thinking that by now I should be used to
it.

I leave the two of them talking and drift into
Mother's bedroom, looking for a pencil and some paper. I see the plaster mold of Mother's teeth, which
she keeps on her dresser. They are from the time she
had to have a porcelain crown made for her molar.

"Why do you keep your teeth on your dresser?"
I've asked.

"Because they are mine," she's answered, as
though it were sufficient reason.

"Is it because you are superstitious, is that why

you save them?" I persist. "Do you think if you throw the mold away, your teeth will all fall out?"

"Don't be silly," she tells me. "I'm a scientist."

"Of course, they're superstitious," Alexandra insists. "Why else would they tie red ribbons on babies' cribs?"

"Well, why else?" I ask my mother.

"It's just a good-luck custom, Ash."

"See," says Alexandra. "Didn't I tell you?"

Mother's slippers are side by side by her bed. I slip one on. It doesn't fit. Mother's feet are very large. "When they were children," Grandma has told me, "they would go about barefoot, or in torn shoes, or wearing sneakers which they could buy from a shelf and not have to try on. They were ashamed of their feet."

"We weren't ashamed," Mother says now. "Having big feet gets you more shoe for your money."

Aunt Elizabeth agrees. "Who was ashamed?" she asks. "If you want better balance, you need bigger feet."

"Small feet look funny," both of them say. "How do they stand on such short feet?" she and Mother ask each other.

"But they did not think that way in their teens,"

Grandma insists. "'What size do you wear?' the salesperson would ask.

"'Size twelve,' they'd barely whisper.

"'Such a big size. Are you sure size twelve? Perhaps I should measure,' the clerk would announce to the rest of the store. 'I'm so sorry,' she'd shout across the floor at them, 'we have nothing in your size. Perhaps a man's shoe. I have a nice-looking loafer. No one would know the difference, believe me.'

"'No, thank you,' they would say, and slink out of the store."

I rejoin them in the living room, where Aunt Elizabeth is reading out loud to Mother. "You have to take good care of your feet, one day we'll all have to run," the podiatrist warns in the book she is reading. She and Mother laugh. The threat seems ready-made for them. They keep their shoes in order, so to speak, and anticipate disaster at every step. Alexandra and I have compared notes. Both our mothers scrutinize their closets monthly, deciding what to take, what not to take.

"Take where, for goodness' sake?" our fathers ask. "Where are you going?"

"Nowhere," they say. "Just in case."

They hide their jewelry in the house. "The banks

would be closed," they explain to each other. "You can always trade gold."

"When?" Alexandra and I used to ask anxiously. "When will the banks be closed?" It comforts me to hear from a book there's someone else who shares their fears. I thought our mothers were the only ones.

"It's too bad your project's finished," Aunt Elizabeth says, putting aside her book, "because I just remembered something." I don't correct her. "It's rude to contradict," I'm often told. Mother says nothing, although she looks surprised.

"When we were children and lived in the city," Aunt Elizabeth says, "your mother and I each slept in a single bed on opposite sides of the room we shared. There was a bookcase on either wall and blue linoleum on the floor. Every night, before we went to sleep, we would take a piece of string, the sort one used to get from bakeries or fish stores. I would hold one end, and your mother would hold the other. That way, even after we had gone to sleep, we felt connected through the night. We did it even when we'd had a fight; even when we hadn't made up yet, we'd hold tightly to that string."

"That's a nice story," I tell her. I think I may use it.

CHAPTER 10

Social Studies, II

I am sitting in Ms. Baxter's class, listening to reports. Well, I am not listening that hard to the reports. I'm mostly waiting for Sylvia's turn to come.

"How come she picked you?" I asked when I first heard. I meant, of course, how come she'd picked Sylvia and hadn't picked me. Sylvia shrugged, not knowing.

"I have selected from the outlines you handed in last week several which seemed of special interest to have read aloud," Ms. Baxter announced at the beginning of class. If Uncle Max's sister's mother-in-law's escape from Russia didn't seem interesting, it's hard to imagine what might. I try to keep an open mind.

"Foot washing," I hear Horace explain to the class, "has never stopped." I wonder where it has never stopped. I think it has never even started here. According to Horace, it's part of the communion service at the Galax Primitive Baptist Church in Galax, Virginia, where his grandmother was a girl. He holds up a book with photographs to show us. Sure enough, there is a picture of a group of people in a church, each one washing some other one's foot.

Horace has a tape recording of a portion of the service, which he plays for us. It tells about how Jesus, when He ended the Passover, broke bread and told His disciples to eat it. Then He took the cup, and they all drank from it. Then Jesus washed the disciples' feet. And that was the first communion. It's in the New Testament, in the Gospel of John. But the Baptist preacher on the tape tells more. One time, he tells, Jesus came into a Pharisee's home. While He was there, a woman came, a sinner, the worst kind of sinner. Well, the Pharisee thought that if Jesus were a real and true prophet, He would see through the woman to the sinner she was. Instead, the woman anointed Jesus' head with oil and, weeping, washed

His feet with her tears, and Jesus turned to Simon the Pharisee and said, "Simon, seest thou this woman?" Well, Simon possibly had 20-20 vision; she was standing right in his presence; he couldn't help seeing the woman. But of course, Jesus meant, see how this woman has anointed me and washed my feet and see how I forgive her her sins. "And that," concludes Horace, "is how foot washing came to be part of the communion service among some Christian sects, including my grandmother's." He turns off the tape.

Naturally, some of us in the class would like to know more. I, for one, would like to know what happened afterward to Simon. "What happened afterward to Simon the Pharisee?" asks Gary.

Horace doesn't know. "I think it wasn't an important part of the story," he says.

Irina's turn is next. As she speaks, she twirls a strand of hair nervously around one finger. "When my mother was twelve," Irina begins, "she lived with her mother in Estonia. They were political refugees from Russia. My mother's only toy, and her most prized possession, was a blue velvet dog she'd been given years before as a birthday gift from her father. Her father, who was alive and well, was temporarily separated from them by the war. My mother cherished that dog. Cherie, she called it.

"One day a cousin, not even a first cousin, came with her mother to visit. The cousin was three, maybe four. The cousin's father had just been killed in the same war that separated my mother from her father. The whole time they stayed, that cousin played with my mother's toy dog.

"As she was leaving on the train, she clutched Cherie in her arms. She did not want to give it back. My grandmother said to my mother, 'Poor child, she has nothing. She has even lost her father. If you give your dog to her now, God will give it back.' My mother let the cousin take the dog. It would be years, she told me, before she would believe in God again.

"Time passed. The Germans reached Estonia. Mother's family fled to Sweden. Mother saw her cousin now and then. Eventually both families left Sweden for America, though not together. My mother was older than the cousin; they moved in different circles; only once in a while would their paths cross.

"More years passed. My mother married. I was born. Then, not long after, the cousin came to visit. She brought with her a cardboard box; in it was the velvet dog to be my birthday gift. 'Everywhere we went,' that cousin said, 'and every place we left, the dog came with us. Coming to America, we carried just two suitcases. The velvet dog was packed in one of them.' My mother says from that day she believed in God again." Irina pauses. "My mother also says that when she told her mother about Cherie and how she got her back, my grandmother said to her, 'I don't remember ever saying that, about God would give it back.' My mother, though, is certain," says Irina. She takes her seat. No one asks her any questions. I make a mental note to ask my father what his father took with him when he left Russia.

Sylvia is next and last. Sylvia Lee who is Chinese-American, but not to me since years before.

"American," she screamed. "I am American like you. How can you be so stupid not to know it?"

"Just like you," Mother confirmed at the time.

"But she looks so different," I answered.

"Different from whom?" my mother asked.

Years ago a man once asked me, "Are you Chinese?" I ran home and asked my mother.

"Am I Chinese? A man just asked me."

"Chinese?" my mother said, seeming put-out by the question. "Why did he think you were Chinese? What was wrong with that man? Haven't I told you not to talk to strangers?"

"He was Chinese," I informed her.

"Who?" she asked.

"The man who asked me. The one who asked was I Chinese. I think he thought I looked like him."

"Oh," Mother said then, dismissing the subject, unconcerned, not wanting it thought that she was prejudiced. Later she repeated the story to my father. "You see," she said, laughing, thinking by then it was a funny story, "it was a Chinese man who asked her."

I did not think it was funny. For weeks afterward I looked in mirrors carefully, tilting my head, examining my face, squinting, practicing to be Chinese in case it ever turned out that I was.

When I was little, other children would sometimes make fun of me and tease. "Fat face," they would say. "You have a fat face."

"Flat face, flat face," they would yell at Sylvia when they were angry with her for whatever reason. Why do they call me flat face? I'd wonder. Not flat face, fat face. "You have a fat face," my third-grade teacher, Miss Armellino, told me once, angry when I couldn't learn to tell the time and didn't seem to care. "She said that to you?" Mother asked. "She really said that?" I was already in junior high school before I could bring myself to tell her.

Sylvia stands in front of the room now, ready to begin her report. She stands very straight so that even though she's just my height, people think she's taller. "What people, Ash?" she asks me. I am certain if she wanted, she could be a fashion model. "Are you crazy, Ash? Stand there smiling for everyone to stare at. Why would I want to do that?"

She waits until everyone is quiet. Even in first grade she could act as much like a grownup as a grownup could. "When I was starting my research," she says, "I happened to see a Chinese-American woman being interviewed on television about a book she'd written. She told the interviewer about her own mother and the stories that she told. The stories her mother told her usually had lessons, terrible lessons. To this day, the author said, she did not know if the stories were the truth or made-up tales. Asking would have been rude. It would have been impossible. 'Are you lying, Mother?' it would have been the same as saying. So she never asked. Instead, she put the stories in her book, which I borrowed from the library. Right away I saw how it could help me with my project."

Sylvia opens the yellow folder she is holding and begins to read. "*The Woman Warrior* by Maxine Hong Kingston. The Chinese-American family in the book includes two girls. Girls were not as good to have as boys to Chinese families, maybe not even to Chinese-American families," reports Sylvia.

"It's nothing to do with Chinese," Leslie interrupts from her seat. "Baby boys are more popular wherever you go."

Maybe, maybe not, I think. I once asked my father didn't he want a boy. "Don't be silly," he told me. "I always wanted girls."

"It is the truth," my mother told her mother, shrugging.

"Why?" I asked him. "Why did you want girls?"

"Because they're smarter," he answered.

I have him there. "If girls are smarter," I asked, "why aren't they president?"

"Becoming president," he told me gravely, "requires a different set of aptitudes entirely."

I turn my attention back to Sylvia, having by now missed much of what she's said. She is explaining that when the third child born in the book is a son, the oldest girl, with good reason, is jealous. "She asks her mother, 'Did you roll an egg on *my* face like that when I was born? Did you have a full month party for *me*? Did you turn on all the lights? Did you send *my* picture to Grandmother? Why not? Because I'm a girl? Is that why not?' It was just that way in my family," says Sylvia.

I am not absolutely positive if Sylvia means by "that way" that she has an older sister and a younger brother, as she does, or that her older sister was jealous just like the sister in the book and asked their mother the same questions, or maybe, I think, she is only making this last part up so that her facts will fit her research.

Bernadette raises her hand. "It's that way in America," she says, "not just if you're a boy but also if you're first. Of course, to be first and a boy is best, but just to be first can be almost as good." Bernadette, who has an older sister, has reason on her side. "Where," she asked her mother, "is *my* engraved silver spoon? Where are all *my* baby photographs? Why did no one bronze *my* shoes or save *my* baby blanket?"

Bernadette tells the class, "It makes me so angry. When I have children," she says, "I will do everything the same for each of them, no matter in what order they're born."

That night I tell my mother about Sylvia's report. "Some Chinese," I explain, "came to this country through California, when they were allowed. They were held on Angel Island. Doctors poked them. Cross-examiners examined them. Detainers detained them, for weeks, sometimes months. There were years when they only sent them back."

"It sounds to me," my mother says, "a lot like Ellis Island." That was why, she reminds me, her grandmother, my great-grandmother, did not come that way.

Not come what way? I wonder. Not come through California? Does she mean she didn't come that way? I already know that.

"It was why she came through Canada," she says, surprising me by something I once knew, but have forgotten.

"Yes," I say, "through Canada, but still, she would have had to pass through immigration. She didn't just stroll across the border, after all."

"Don't be silly," Mother says. "She came on a train, with my Uncle Moe and my Aunt Molly. Only your grandmother was born in this country. She was the youngest. It made her special."

"Being youngest made her special?"

"Oh, Ash, it made her special being born American. She didn't have to be made into a citizen. By the time her father got his papers, with Moe's and Molly's names included, she was already one."

"Yes," I insist, going back to the start, "but there still must have been guards at the border, doctors to poke her. Didn't they roll back her eyelids, try to get her to cough?"

My mother shrugs. "It's not the way I heard it."

Before I fall asleep that night I lie in bed and think about my project. I think about my grandmother and about her mother. I also think about Sylvia.

One time, years ago, when Sylvia was visiting, my grandmother was visiting, too. She admired Sylvia's hair. Later, after Sylvia had gone home, my grandmother said to me, "You know, Chinese hair, it doesn't hurt when you pull it."

I looked at her, amazed. "How do you know that?" I asked. I can never seem to stop myself in time from asking her how she know things I know she does not know, things that are not so.

"Once," she said, "there was a girl living in our neighborhood. She was Chinese. She had long black braids. They were just like your friend's braids. We would pull on them, and she would say, 'Go ahead, pull. It doesn't hurt me.' No matter how hard we pulled, it would never make her cry."

"Why did you pull her hair?" I asked. "Did she do something bad to you?"

"Oh, no," Grandma said. "She was our friend."

"I see," I said, though of course I didn't.

"My mother," continued my grandmother, "your great-grandmother, asked her one time, 'Is it just your hair that doesn't hurt, or is it all Chinese hair?'

"'All Chinese hair,' she told us. 'You can pull Chinese hair forever, and it will not hurt.'"

I told Alexandra about Grandma's story. "It goes to show," I said, "you can't believe everything that Grandma tells you."

"The point is," Alexandra said, "you can't believe everything that anybody tells you."

CHAPTER 11

The Grandmother from Poland

Mother is in the kitchen cooking for herself. The reason she is cooking for herself and not for us is we don't eat what Mother cooks. "What made you think of that?" Father asked that time when she put chocolate in the bread.

Mother shrugged. "It seemed a good idea." The next morning she wrapped both loaves and took them to work.

"It's interesting bread," one of her colleagues said. Mother took it as a compliment.

Right now she's preparing an omelet for her dinner. Eggs and broccoli are cooking in the pan. Besides, there are three kinds of cheese, onions, peppers, herbs, and sesame seeds. Mother is a vegetarian, although she occasionally eats fish.

"Fish," Grandma likes to point out to her, "is not a vegetable."

"So sue me," I have heard Mother say under her breath. Out loud she says, "I guess I'm just a vegetarian who eats fish, sometimes."

Father is the family chef when he is home. Tonight he's at a conference. Mother does not care for conferences and will not go to them. "No one cares for them," Father explains to her. "Attendance sometimes is required." Mother doesn't see it that way.

"It's interesting," I tell her, attempting conversation, "you don't cook, and your mother doesn't cook. I guess it runs in the family." Mother gives me a funny look.

"I'm cooking this minute," she says.

"Yes, but I mean, usually you don't. Did Grandpa cook when you were little?"

"Cocoa," she says. "He made delicious cocoa."

I do not remember my grandfather Hofstaedter that well. He had a heart attack when I was nine. I do remember he could whistle.

"That man was some whistler," Mother says.

"It's a shame that none of us inherited his talent."
She means, of course, his musical talent in general
and not just his whistle. "Ashley sings the way I do,"
Mother sometimes jokes. "They both sing just the
way we do," Aunt Elizabeth confirms, including
Alexandra. "Tone-deaf," I told the music teacher in
fifth grade. "It runs in my family."

"No one," she informed me, authoritatively, if
unreliably, "is actually tone-deaf. Sometimes people
think they are because they have not received the
proper training and encouragement." She encour-
aged me. I tried.

"Some people," Mother pointed out when she
heard me practicing at home, "are not cut out for
singing. I myself," she said, "am a listener. You
know, Ash, without listeners, there'd be no point in
singers."

"You know, Ashley," my music teacher said at
last, "I am certain you could learn in time, but the
problem is the winter concert will be here before we
know it." She taught me how to turn the pages while
she played the piano for the singers.

"You did fine, Ash," Mother said proudly the
evening of the concert. "You have such wonderful
posture."

I return to the topic at hand. "If Grandma didn't

cook, and Grandpa made cocoa, who made dinner in your house?"

"As I recall," says Mother, "we all took turns." That, I think, must have been interesting. "Of course, when I was very young," Mother continues, "my grandmother lived with us, and she did the cooking." This, it will turn out, is the same grandmother who came to America from Poland on a train from Canada. I am surprised to hear she ever lived with them. Why, I wonder, did no one ever tell me this before?

"It is like that in this family," Alexandra explains. "It wasn't until after our mothers were born that Grandpa ever thought to mention both his parents had been twins. Twins ran in his family."

"I didn't know twins ran in families."

"Ashley," Alexandra says, sighing, "you're missing the point."

"Was she a good cook?" I ask my mother now, meaning, of course, her grandmother.

"Not that I remember," Mother says. "Everything she ever served was boiled. Still, she knew some things."

"Like what?" I ask.

"For one thing," Mother answers, "she could predict the weather. 'Rain today,' she'd say some sunny morning. 'Don't forget your boots, girls.' Of course we did. She'd be waiting for us outside school, holding our umbrellas. 'Look at your shoes, girls, ruined,' she'd scold. One time Aunt Elizabeth asked her why she hadn't brought our boots along with the umbrellas. 'It's to teach you a lesson,' she yelled. Of course, she yelled it in Yiddish."

"Yiddish? How did you understand what she was saying?"

"I spoke Yiddish then," my mother tells me.

"You spoke Yiddish?" I ask, amazed. "Can you speak it now?"

"Maybe a little. I haven't used it in years."

"Say something in Yiddish, please," I beg.

Mother shrugs. "Grandma Katia used to look at us, at Aunt Elizabeth and me, and say, 'Such *shayna meydlakh, keyn-ayen-hore.*' I always thought that she was saying, 'Such shining girls, God bless them.' What she was really saying was, 'Such pretty girls, may the evil eye look elsewhere.'"

"She believed in evil eyes?"

"It was just an expression," says Mother, "something to say. Anyway, I liked thinking of myself as being a shining girl. It made me feel special."

"What else?" I ask my mother, meaning, what else does she remember about her grandmother?

"That she was poor," my mother says. "I remember that. Especially in Poland. Once, when Aunt Elizabeth and I decided we each wanted our own bedroom and shouldn't have to share, she told us when she was our age, she hadn't even had her own bed. 'I shared with four sisters,' she said, 'so who are you to complain?' We asked her how five could fit in one bed. 'Five couldn't,' she'd answered. 'Only four could fit at one time. The fifth had to stand. We rotated. Every night one of us got to stay up until morning.'"

"Is that story true?" I ask.

Mother doesn't know. "I do know, though," she tells me, "your great-grandmother was poor all her life. Even after she came to America, she was still poor. She had been living here only two years when a building fell on her husband and killed him. He had come here before them. When she arrived by train with Molly and Moe, they were coming to join him.

"So," Mother says, "there she was, a widow with three children and a parrot. There wasn't even a bathtub in their apartment. They'd set a basin in the kitchen by the stove that was almost just as good. Your great-grandmother spoke hardly any English. Even her parrot spoke only Yiddish. Fortunately she was an excellent cardplayer. Well, she did take in boarders and occasional sewing, and that paid the rent, but it was her cardplaying that got them all by.

It was she who taught your Aunt Elizabeth and me to play. 'A waste of time,' said our mother, who disapproved of cards. She never noticed your great-grandmother was a gambler."

"How could she not have noticed?" I ask. "It was her own mother, after all."

Mother smiles. "Aunt Elizabeth believes Grandma has repressed that portion of her childhood. Had she known that Aunt Elizabeth and I played cards for money, as your great-grandmother taught us, she would have hit the ceiling. 'Criminals,' she would have called us. 'I'm raising a couple of card sharks.'

"It was your great-grandmother who was the card shark, though I always did suspect that parrot had a lot to do with her exceptional good luck. It sat on her shoulder when she played and whispered in her ear. I always thought it must be telling her what cards were in the other players' hands. After it had eaten the paint from its cage and died, it seemed to me she didn't win so often. Oh, how Grandma Katia cried. 'It's unseemly,' said our mother, 'to carry on that way about a bird.'"

Mother has eaten her omelet, and I have finished yesterday's leftover chicken and peas. "I wonder whose turn it is to wash dishes," says Mother. No one answers.

"It reminds me of a story," she says, "a Polish story."

She begins it.

"Several cooks were in a kitchen, cooking, when the girl next door came by.

" 'Lend a hand?' they asked her.

" 'Oh, I'd like to, but I haven't brought an apron. I'd get mussed.' So instead, she sat and watched them work and traded stories with them. Dinnertime came.

" 'Who'd like a piece of buttered bread?' asked one.

" 'Oh, I would,' said the girl, and ate it.

" 'Who'd like a glass of ale?' another asked.

" 'Oh, I would,' said the girl, and drank it.

" 'There are dishes to be washed; who'll wash them?' asked a third. No one said a word. At last the girl spoke up.

" 'Speak up,' she told the others. 'It isn't right for me always to be first to answer.' "

Mother and I do dishes together. I wash, and she dries. "Thank you," we tell each other when we're finished.

Father's Side of the Family

Today Father came home carrying a violin. To say that it surprised me would be to understate the situation vastly.

"I got it for a bargain," he explained.

"Yes, a bargain, but what is it for?" asked Mother.

"To play," he said. "What else?" Then he removed it from its case, tuned and played it. He played it beautifully. Father, it turns out, is some musician. "It runs in my family."

"What runs in your family?" asks Mother.

"Fiddling," says Father. "We're all of us wonderful fiddlers."

"I see," says Mother. "I'm surprised you never mentioned it before."

"Yes," says Father, seeming to agree. "My own father," he adds, "always hoped I'd grow up to be a concert violinist. Our fiddles were the main things he packed when we were coming to America."

At least, I think, I know the answer to the question: "What was it that your father took when he left Russia?"

"We?" questions Mother, always quicker than I to catch a discrepancy in one of Father's narratives. "Who is this 'we' that came to America?"

Father clears his throat. Then he plays a few notes on his fiddle. "Remember the story I told for Ashley's report, about picking up the bull and saving kopeks and catching chicken pox in Russia? Well, I changed it just a little when I told it."

"Really," Mother answers noncommittally.

"Yes," Father says. "Naturally it happened, but not exactly as I said. I was the one who had to get strong, not my father. My father was strong enough already. He could hold his fiddle with just one hand and, with his other, carry me."

"If this is a joke," says Mother, "it isn't *that* funny."

"It isn't a joke," says Father, and his eyes do not glint as they do when he's telling a story.

"I can still recall the way it was. I was just a baby at the time. I remember it," he says, "as if it happened yesterday. There I was, warm in my blanket, held securely in my father's arm. The sea was very rough. Everybody on the ship but me was seasick." His eyes are glinting now.

"I'll bet," says Mother. "Is there some special reason," she inquires, "you've never brought this up before?"

"No special reason," Father says.

Years later I am a grownup applying for a passport. Where were your parents born? I have to answer on the form. America, I write, without thinking. Both my parents are American. Russia does not even seem a possibility.

"When we arrived in New York," Father continues, "you can imagine we were poor. Well, we weren't *that* poor. At least we had a bathtub."

If it were left to me to choose, I think I'd sooner have a parrot, but I don't interrupt to say so.

"When I was twelve," says Father, "I went to work in Coney Island. Do you know Coney Island?" he asks, looking at me.

Well, I know *about* Coney Island. "It was a place that had carnival rides," I say, "in Brooklyn."

"Yes, carnival rides," he says, "and more. I would stand outside a tent and play my violin. When enough people lined up, we'd all start shouting. Esther and Sam worked with me; you know my cousins Esther and Sam?"

"What did you shout?" I ask.

" 'Step right up, step right up. Inside this tent for just ten cents you'll see the most exciting, most spectacular, most phenomenal sights that you have ever seen,' " Father shouts.

"Then what?"

"Then people would pay their dimes and go inside the tent. It was a freak show."

"I would have thought," says Mother, "your father would have had more sense than to let you do that."

"What sense?" says Father. "We needed the money, the same as the midgets. It was all that we knew how to do."

"Especially," Mother continues calmly, "considering your own mother was almost a dwarf."

"What do you mean," I ask, " 'almost a dwarf'?" I appeal to Father. "What does she mean?" His mother died when he was small, so of course, I never saw her.

"Short," he explains. "My mother was extremely short."

Naturally we have no photographs of her. Other families, I point out, have photographs.

"Don't be silly, Ashley," Mother says. "If you are coming here from somewhere else by boat, carrying everything you own on just your back, photographs might not be high on your list of things to pack."

"The fiddles seemed more important at the time," says Father.

"Why," I ask Cousin Esther on one of her rare visits to our house, "aren't there any photographs?"

"From photographs I don't remember," she replies. "But the rooster your father had when we were living in the Bronx, him I remember. Who could forget such a pet?"

"A rooster?" I ask. "How did Father come to have a rooster in the Bronx?"

"He got it in the first place from Aunt Fanny, your great-aunt Fanny," Cousin Esther says. "Probably she meant for us to eat it when she brought it. But no one in our family ever did."

"Do people eat roosters?" I ask. Chickens, ducks, cornish hens, these I know about. "I've never seen a rooster in the store."

"Sure they're in the store," says Cousin Esther. "Only they don't say 'rooster.' They say 'chicken.'

Most chickens they sell are young roosters. Chickens they keep on the farm to lay eggs. Where have you been you don't know that? Anyway, that particular rooster your father made into a pet."

"So what happened to it?" I ask. Of course, I mean eventually.

"Roosters are not really city birds," Cousin Esther explains. "They're very noisy. The neighbors did not care for it. One day they kidnapped it. A delegation came and told your grandfather they had sent it to the country. 'A rooster,' they said, 'belongs in the country. He'll be happier there.'

"Your father, it goes without saying, was not happy when he heard it. He also didn't believe it. Both of us believed, instead, the neighbors had kidnapped, cooked, and eaten it. For all we knew, they'd had a dinner party."

I can't imagine having rooster for a dinner party, but then I have never understood their taste in food. "What part is that?" I used to ask, pointing, before I knew better. I have watched them eat lung stew, spiced tongue, calves'-foot jelly; everybody wants the chicken neck. Even Grandmother Hofstaedter will go out of her way for a stuffed chicken neck. I do not wonder Mother became a vegetarian.

Cousin Esther, it turns out, knows more about roosters than just about Father's. "Oh, yes," she says, "pet roosters go way back. I'll tell you a story.

"There was a poor woman in Russia one time who had a pet rooster. A little rooster it was, and Little Rooster she called it. She would put it out in her yard to find its own food.

"Well, one time it could find nothing to eat, so it walked down the road to try its luck there. It scratched and it scratched, until wonder of wonders, it scratched up a diamond button. Just at that minute it happened that the Russian czar came by with all of his servants.

"When the czar saw the rooster with the diamond button, naturally he wanted it. But the rooster told him, No. That rooster was planning to take the diamond button home to give to his poor mistress. 'She likes diamond buttons,' the rooster told the czar.

"Well, the czar liked diamond buttons himself. He ordered a servant to catch the rooster and take the diamond button from him, and the servant did. Then they all went away home, and the czar had the diamond button put with all the other Russian jewels in the jewel room in the palace.

"The rooster was not pleased. He made his way to the palace and called for his button. 'Cock-a-doodle-do, give me back my diamond button,' he crowed. It made the czar angry.

"He ordered a servant to catch the rooster and throw him into the well. 'Let him drown.'

"The servant caught the rooster and threw him into the well. But the rooster drank up all the water and never drowned at all. Instead, he flew back to the palace, and once more he crowed, 'Cock-a-doodle-do, give me back my diamond button.'

"It made the czar even angrier than he had been before. He ordered another servant to catch the rooster and this time to throw him into the fire. 'Let him burn.'

"The servant did. But the rooster let out all the water he had swallowed from the well, put out the fire, and never burned at all. He went back again to the czar. 'Cock-a-doodle-do,' he crowed a third time. 'Give me back my diamond button.'

"It made the czar angrier than ever. Again he called a servant. He ordered him to catch the rooster and this time throw him into a beehive to be stung, and the servant did.

"But as with the water, the rooster only swallowed all the bees and was never stung at all. He flew back to the palace. 'Cock-a-doodle-do,' he crowed. 'Give me back my diamond button.'

"The czar was so angry now he didn't know what to do. 'What shall I do? What shall I do?' he cried.

"Finally, he did the only thing that he could think of doing, which goes to show he should have thought some more. He had the rooster captured and he sat on it. Well, of course, no sooner did he do that than the rooster let all the bees out of his stomach, and did they ever sting the czar!

"'Ouch, ouch, ouch,' he cried, although naturally," says Cousin Esther, "he cried it in Russian. 'Take this rooster to the jewel room,' the czar told his servants, 'and let him find his diamond button.'

"So the servants took the rooster to the jewel room, and they told him, 'Find your diamond button.' But the same as with the water and the bees, the rooster swallowed not only his own diamond button, which he quickly found, but all the jewels in the jewel room. Then he waddled home as fast as he could, let all the jewels out of his stomach and gave them to the poor woman whose pet he was. You can imagine she was pleased. Then the rooster went back out into the yard to look for his dinner."

That night, after Cousin Esther has gone home, I sit in my room at my desk and take a deep breath. Am I not a bearer of family tradition as much as anybody else? Didn't Alexandra read that to me from a book? And isn't it the truth that telling stories runs in my family? Who am I to tamper with tradition, and if

I don't start now, then when? I pick up my pencil and begin. "My Father's Side of the Family," I print carefully at the top of the page.

> My father and his family came from Russia. They were Jewish, but they lived like Gypsies. Jewish Gypsies, I guess you'd call them. They traveled in a caravan. It was a small caravan, big enough for just one family and a bear. Grandma had found the bear asleep in the woods, beside a chimpanzee. It was a baby at the time. The chimpanzee, she'd said, seemed happy to relinquish responsibility for it.
> This was the grandmother who was a dwarf, who played the violin. They all played violins. It was how they earned their living. Except for the bear. The bear would dance to the tunes they played.
> Grandma, besides being a dwarf and a fiddler, was also a jeweler. She made cunning articles of gold and silver. It was because of this a band of bandits one time tried to kidnap her and take her with them. It is a Russian superstition that dwarfs who work in metal bring good luck. You couldn't have proved it by my grandmother. Also, the bandits had not counted on the bear, who, together with Grandma, ran all of them off. But after that, Grandma never felt the same again about life on the road. Besides, my father, like the bear, was growing up.
> "The Russian countryside," said Grandma,

"may be fine for a bear, but it's no place to bring up a boy." So they said good-bye to the bear, although it made them sad to do so, and took a boat to New York. Being Jewish Gypsies in Russia was anyway hard, and in America they had heard a child could grow up to be someone.

Becoming someone *in* America, of course, was one thing; getting *to* America was another. They did not understand the system, so much paper work. But if there is one thing Jewish Gypsies are, it is resourceful. Therefore, they dressed my father as a midget. It was a very good disguise. He was only five. Grandpa wore a bear suit and carried the fiddles.

"We're a circus act," they said at the border. "We were separated from our caravan." That much at least was the truth. The border guard believed them. He waved them through. "Hey, that's some bear," was all that he said. Of course, he said it in English, so they were never absolutely certain.

I show the story to my father.

"Nice," he says, smiling. "Of course, you know, it's not exactly how it happened."

"No?" I ask. "Are you sure? Are you sure it didn't happen just that way? Maybe you forgot. After all," I point out, "it was a long time ago."

"Yes," Father says, "a long time ago. I suppose it could have happened that way. I mean, it could have happened almost that way, except for one thing. My mother never made the trip. Your grandmother died in Russia of influenza that turned into pneumonia. It was right after that my father packed our bags, the fiddles, and me, and took the boat from Russia. There was no penicillin then. Had there been, it might have been a different story altogether."

"I'm sorry," I say. "I didn't know that."

"How could you know it? It was a long time ago. Don't be sorry, Ash," says Father. "I like your version better."

CHAPTER 13

Jascha

W ell, that's that. My paper's handed in. I've got my grade. I got a check. Well, everybody got a check.

"It isn't fair," I complained.

"Of course, it isn't fair. You're in high school, not in fair school," Bernadette explained.

Irina almost had a fit. "My toy dog survived the Russians and the Germans, not to mention war. What can she mean by a check!"

"You all did very well," Ms. Baxter said,

handing back our papers. "Family history is not a contest, after all." A nice time, I think, for her to tell us.

"It sounds like a good way to look at it to me," says Mother. "By the way, there's a letter for you on the kitchen table. It's from Grandpa."

First-class mail is almost an event. I go downstairs to get it. It's close to dinnertime. Father is in the kitchen, clanking pots, running water, fixing supper. I take my letter into the living room to read it.

Dear Ashley,

When you telephoned to ask about my flying, you said if I should think of something longer, I should write it. Well, I did, and I did. Jascha is longer. Much too long to tell you on the telephone long distance. If I were you, Ash, I think I might sit down to read this.

I sit down.

Jascha [I continue reading] was your father's older brother when we lived in Russia. Well, I'm not surprised if you have never heard of him. For all I know, your father's never even mentioned life in Russia to you. Your father, Ash, is very secretive. He gets it from his mother. Keeping secrets ran in her family. All of them kept secrets. Well, to tell the truth, in Russia keeping secrets wasn't such a bad idea. It was much safer.

Nevertheless, I always did think they carried it to unusual extremes. Take, for example, my wife. Until Jascha was born, I never even knew her real name was Rosalie. "I always thought it was Rose," I said. "Are you sure Rosalie?"

"Sure I'm sure," she answered. "Rose is for short. It's just what they call me."

"Well, sure," I told her, "a short name for a short person, what could be better?" Well, it was the wrong thing to say. Never make jokes, Ashley, about a short person's height, I will tell you that. They won't appreciate it. "So let it be Rosalie," I said, which is neither here nor there. The point of this letter is Jascha.

For a family history project, Ashley, you should put in your whole family. Jascha was certainly family, a beautiful child. Well, a little on the short side, even for five, but otherwise perfect. Already at five, that child was some fiddler. In America, he might have been a concert violinist. Probably also, he would have been called Joseph.

As it was, he never made it through the influenza epidemic. Well, neither did his mother. Those were terrible times, Ash. Be glad you didn't live then. I wish, though, your grandmother could have known you. She would have been so proud. Well, I'm sure she's proud now. So Ash, put Jascha and his mother in your paper. Put that they were

family. And about that time I flew, don't worry.
Nowadays, if you want, I hear they give lessons.

Love,
Grandpa

I stand up slowly and go into the kitchen.
"Jascha! How could you have never told me?" Father
looks at me in surprise. He sees the letter I am
waving in the air. He's good at putting two and two
together.

"To tell the truth, Ash," he says mildly, "I'd almost forgotten him myself. It was a long time ago. I
was just a baby when he died. Be glad," he says after
a while, "I got the boat ride right." It doesn't strike
me funny.

"It isn't funny," I say.

Father frowns. "You may be right." He wrinkles
his forehead, making his eyeglasses shift until they
are sitting crookedly on his nose. "I do seem to recall," he says finally, "a photograph that Grandpa
kept for years on a stand beside his cello when we
were living in the Bronx. I'm pretty sure it was of
Jascha."

"A photograph? I thought that you didn't bring
photographs from Russia."

Father shrugs. "We didn't, except, I guess, for

that one." Well, sure, I think. Sure, there would have had to be a photograph. Wasn't Jascha the oldest? The oldest boy. Just as Sylvia had said; they take pictures of the oldest son. "Jascha was dead," my father says. "I guess Grandpa couldn't bear, after all, to leave all his memories in Russia."

Mother has come into the kitchen. She's looking at both of us now. "Excuse me," she says, "but what cello?"

I can't imagine what she's talking about. It turns out Father can.

"My father used to play the cello," he explains. "Sure," he says, "he was a virtuoso."

"I thought," Mother says, "all of you were fiddlers."

"Well, sure, fiddlers," says Father, "but there's more to fiddling than only violins. I thought everybody knew that."

"I see," says Mother.

All I see is all my theories of Father as an only child are wrong. He wasn't only, wasn't oldest, wasn't special. No wonder there are no photographs of him. All he was was last.

Much later that evening I sit in my room, Luther, the cat, in my lap, and try to sort things out. Luther purrs and kneads my terry-cloth robe with his claws. He seems deliriously happy to be with me.

I think back to years ago when I was small. If I had seen a scary movie or been frightened by a fairy tale, Mother used to say to reassure me, "Don't be afraid, Ashley, it's only a story." I was never reassured. Father's way was better. "If you don't like the ending, Ash, then change it," he'd advise. I hear him downstairs, tuning his violin. I lean back in my chair and listen. He is playing a mazurka, a happy dancing song. Father plays with feeling. I let the sounds play over me. "Well, sure," I explain to my cat, "it isn't so bad being last. The ones who are last get to make up the stories."

NOTES AND SOURCES

The stories in this book are original, and the characters imagined, with the following exceptions:

The creation myth in Chapter 4 is from a South American Indian source and variously told in other places.

The mandrake root story, also in Chapter 4, is a well-known legend. Mandrake is, in fact, a poisonous form of nightshade that has a forked root. It does not grow in northern Europe, where the legend is believed to have originated. It was, however, imported into Germany, and people who owned the root, or roots of similar plants, reportedly took excellent care of them, wrapping them in velvet and silk, washing them carefully, and so on to assure their own wealth, power, and happiness. The version I include is based on the one found in Donald Ward, ed. *The German Legends of the Brothers Grimm*, Vol. I (Philadelphia: Institute for the Study of Human Issues, 1981), pages 93–94.

The "Sandbox," also in Chapter 4, is an adaptation of a story, "The Sandbox Story," which appears in Steven J. Zeitlin, Amy J. Kotkin, and Holly Cutting Baker, eds., *A Celebration of American Family Folklore: Tales and Traditions from the Smithsonian's Collection* (New York: Pantheon, 1982), pages 134–35. It was told by Pat Matlock, Washington, D.C., as one of a series she recalled her father had made up to tell to her and her brother. Interestingly, the stories he made up usually had both children in them, but the one she remembered best was the one in which her brother "doesn't figure at all."

The story Uncle Max tells in Chapter 5 about Eva Feldman actually happened to her. She told it to my sister Eloise Porte, who told it to me. Eva Feldman was the grandmother of my sister's husband, and she was in her nineties when my sister taped her story.

The book Sylvia lends Ashley in Chapter 7, is Richard and Laurna Tallman, *Country Folks: A Handbook for Student Folklore Collectors* (Arkansas: Arkansas College Folklore Archive Publications, 1978).

Stories about magic pots (Chapter 7), exist in many cultures.

"You have to take good care of your feet, one day we'll all have to run," Chapter 9, is a quotation from Gail Godwin's novel *A Mother and Two Daughters* (New York: Viking, 1982).

The story about foot washing in Chapter 10 has been adapted from Lyntha Scott Eiler, Terry Eiler, and Carl Fleischhauer, *Blue Ridge Harvest: A Region's Folklore in Photographs* (Washington, D.C.: Government Printing Office, 1981), pages 63–67. The story was part of a lesson on the meaning of foot washing given by Elder Horace E. Walker at the annual communion service at the Galax Primitive Baptist Church in Galax, Virginia, on August 13, 1978.

The story about the velvet dog, also in that chapter, really happened. It was told by Irene Ilves in September, 1983, at a workshop on Family Folklore, Preserving the Stories of the Past, conducted by Dr. Meg Hodgkin Lippert, during the Everychild

Conference in New York City, sponsored by the Children's Book Council.

The section in Chapter 10 in which the oldest girl in the family questions her mother about birth customs was taken directly from Maxine Hong Kingston, *The Woman Warrior: Memoirs of a Girlhood Among Ghosts* (New York: Knopf, 1977).

Keyn-ayen-hore, a Yiddish word mentioned in Chapter 11, was frequently invoked by my own, and other people's, grandmothers, pronounced and used in various ways. It originates from the Hebrew *ayen hore*, meaning "the eye of evil." *Keyn-ayen-hore* is used in Yiddish as we would use "knock on wood" in English.

The story about the cooks, also in Chapter 11, is based on a Polish peasant tale, "The Sly Gypsy," which appears in Lucia Merecka Borski, ed., *Good Sense and Good Fortune and Other Polish Folk Tales* (New York: David McKay, 1970), pages 66–67.

The story about the rooster and the diamond button in Chapter 12 is an Eastern European folktale, adapted from a version in Kate Seredy, *The Good Master* (New York: Viking, 1935), pages 122–27.